Life

By

Design

~A NOVEL~

ELIZABETH JAMES

DESIGN SERIES #2

Edited by Kathy Krick

DEDICATION

To Sissy and Bobby- I am blessed to have two very special angels watching out for me. I love and miss you.

It started with sunflowers....

THANK YOUS:

There are so many people I want to thank but first and foremost, my husband. I love you and I appreciate your letting me follow my dream.

I also want to thank my mom and dad for being the best support a person could have and the rest of my family for being there for me.

I want to thank my best friends who are all in my heart and still hidden in my book...you know who you are. I love ya'll.

I want to once again recognize my right hand woman, Kassie Baker who has helped me turn this into something really special. Thank you for your endless hours of beta reading and encouragement. I love you...we're a family, remember?

To Kathy Krick...you became my friend and then my editor...I couldn't ask for a better arrangement. Thank you for all your hard work.

To my beta readers, Jodi Negri, Rachael McClusky, and Jemma Scarry...you girls were honest and your feedback rocked. I love you girls!

I also want to thank my E. James Street Team for their tireless efforts to promote and support me! I love my lovely street peeps!

Chapter 1

He proposed! I'm speechless, he proposed. I didn't know he was going to do it tonight, but I knew it was going to be sooner or later. It was expected, I guess, but it still caught me off guard. The Happy Birthday song had just ended. He got down on one knee and gave the most heartfelt proposal I'd ever heard. I stared at Justin and held my breath. With just a moment's hesitation, he got his response. Callie said, "Yes!"

I jumped up, grabbed Callie, and squealed. I was careful not to squeeze baby Brisson but had to show my bestie some love. She was squealing too, and we both jumped up and down like total nuts. Justin stood there looking at us, with his eyebrows raised, and I realized that he might want to kiss his woman, so I stepped away. I felt something yanking on my pant leg and realized Jolene was now squealing. This was right up her alley, being as loud as possible in a public place. I didn't get mad though. She looked so happy and really didn't know what we were excited about. Jay stood and shook Justin's hand to congratulate him and gave Callie a kiss on the cheek. Callie's mom, Leslie was bawling while Tony, Callie's new stepdad, was beaming. Justin's parents, Joe and Dianne, were next in line to hug them and I watched wishing it was happening to me. Now, don't get me wrong, I wasn't jealous. They were so lucky. I dreamed of having parents who loved me and a handsome man who wanted to marry me. I had neither. Apparently, I must have been frowning because Callie caught my eye and mouthed, 'I love you Sis.' She knew just how to get me. I couldn't help but smile. She and I were closer than sisters and since neither of us had any siblings, it was an even closer bond.

In reality, I didn't have any family to speak of. They existed but not in my life. They abandoned me when I moved from my hometown of Portland to follow my boyfriend Tyler. He was my first love, and I thought we'd be together forever. I was wrong. He'd gotten a job offer in Asheville at a construction company with a friend of a friend and convinced me to move with him. My family told me he was "good for nothing" that I'd end up "barefoot and pregnant." I loved him so much I turned my back on them and that was the end of all communication.

We moved into a little apartment and knowing we needed money for rent, I went out and found a job. Thank God I'd taken courses in school that gave me enough experience to get a position working with Callie Brandon at the Mathewson Group. Within a few months of arriving in North Carolina, Tyler lost his job because he quit showing up for work. It seems he was too busy partying with his new friends and couldn't find time to squeeze in a workday. I kept working to support us hoping he'd get his head straight. He didn't. He'd started drinking then taking drugs and nothing I said seemed to matter. He'd say, "Baby, I'm not hooked on this stuff. I can quit anytime I want." Unfortunately, anytime never came.

I got pregnant. I didn't mean for it to happen. I was still on probation at work, and my insurance hadn't started, so I couldn't afford to be on birth control. I tried to remind Tyler we needed to be careful but it didn't seem to matter. Then, the pee stick turned blue. That was the day my life changed. I remember it like it was yesterday. I took the test praying the whole time it wouldn't be positive knowing we weren't ready to be parents but when it was, a sense of calm came over me. I'd pictured the little baby growing inside me, and I knew it was going to be okay. Since I'd taken the test before work, I hid it in the back of the medicine cabinet with the intention of telling Tyler when he got home from whatever he was doing that day.   I was an emotional wreck as I sat at my desk going over my speech in my mind. 'Tyler, we're pregnant.' 'Tyler, the test was positive.' 'Tyler, you're going to be a daddy.' Callie sensed something was wrong and asked me about it. Afraid I'd become a blubbering mess, I lied telling her it was nothing. That night when I got home, I noticed there were no lights on in the apartment. Normally, Tyler would have had four or five of his loser buddies over for a party, but it was quiet. Too quiet. I cautiously walked in and instantly noticed things were missing. I thought we'd been robbed. I took a quick inventory of the few valuable things we owned and quickly realized that the only things missing were his. I wandered into the kitchen and then I saw the note stuck to the refrigerator with a magnet.

Jane, I saw the pregnancy thing in the cabinet. You aren't gonna trap me with some kid. I'm out.

I felt tingles all over as if I were going to pass out. I managed to call Callie because I really didn't have anyone else. She came right over and sat holding my hand until I cried myself dry. She'd had my back ever since.

I jumped as I felt a touch on my arm, bringing me back to reality.

"You ok, Jane?" Callie said looking at me closely. "What's up?"

Shaking my head to clear it, I realized I had tears running down my cheeks. Thinking fast I said, "I'm just so happy for you." I gave her a weak smile. Callie grabbed me and hugged me tight.

"Liar, you look sad," she whispered in my ear. "I know you better than that."

I couldn't lie to her, not anymore. She'd been so good to me. "I was just thinking about Tyler and how my life could have been so different."

"Tyler?" Jay said right behind me. Oh crap. Jay had never heard Jolene's father's real name, only knew him as deadbeat dad. Now I had to explain. This was something I never wanted to have to deal with.

"Tyler is Jolene's...um...biological father," I said cringing saying it out loud.

Jay's eyes narrowed and his jaw tightened. "I see. It has a name." He turned and looked at Jolene who was happily coloring with Leslie and Dianne. "And your life would be different, how?"

I could tell this was upsetting him. "It doesn't mean better Jay, just different. Tyler left before Jolene was even born, and I sometimes wish she had a daddy," I said being as honest as I could be. As I looked at her, I saw Tyler's eyes. He has gorgeous blue eyes and Jolene's were a perfect match. I turned back and I saw a peculiar look on Jay's face. It was gone just as quickly.

"Well, he chose to walk away. It would've been different if you'd kept her from him," he said abruptly. He seemed very angry. Moments later, Jolene jumped up from the table and ran to him grabbing his hand.

"Jay, can you take me to see the fishies?" She said batting her eyelashes and working those blue eyes. His anger faded quickly. Looking down at her with a smile, he nodded. "Yay, Mama! We're gonna see the fishies!" I watched them walk away and could hear her chattering across the restaurant until they stood in front of the giant fish tank.

"What's going on with you two?" Callie asked. She'd seen the entire exchange and obviously saw Jay's tension. "Are things any better? Has he made any moves yet?"

I was about to answer when I saw Justin walking toward us, so I shushed her. "We'll talk later. I can't talk about it right now," I whispered. She smiled a knowing smile and gave me a wink as Justin wrapped his arms around her putting his hands on her tummy. I knew she was thinking there were some juicy details but honestly, there weren't any to tell. Jay and I'd been out to dinner a few times but it was very "friendly". We always took Jolene and usually ended up sitting together near the ball pit at Chuck E. Cheese, which just didn't scream romantic.

I started to wonder if I just wasn't his type. One night, however, he'd stayed for a little while after taking us out to dinner. I'd tucked Jolene in bed and we were sitting next to each other on the couch watching "The Notebook", which he'd never seen. He'd moved to stretch and ended up putting his arm behind me, resting it on my shoulders. I felt him lightly stroke my hair and then twirl it around his fingers. Honestly, it got me all tingly. We'd gotten to the part in the movie where Noah and Allie were getting drenched by the rain and couldn't hold back their love. They kissed. I felt Jay shift a little closer, and I looked over to see him studying me with an intense look that made me melt. He leaned toward me until we were inches apart, and I held my breath. Instinctively, I licked my lips knowing this was finally THE move. Our lips were just about to touch when suddenly I heard a shriek from Jolene's room. Startled, we both jumped up and ran to her room only to find her dangling off her bed. I grabbed her and scooted her safely back on the bed as Jay looked to see what she'd been after. Her Rapunzel doll had somehow tumbled off and she'd tried to grab it without getting out of bed. Tucking her back in, Jay gave her the doll and we both gave her another kiss. We walked out of her room and Jay suddenly yawned. He made the excuse it was a work night, and he headed towards the door. He hugged me and told me goodnight. I was so disappointed. He'd seemed distant again and it was very confusing. I went to bed alone, again.

My daydreaming was interrupted by Jolene's excited voice. "Mama, I saw the fishies! They had lots and lots of them!" She was practically bouncing. I looked over at the table and saw she'd had cake AND soda. Oh boy! She was going to be wired for hours. I glanced down at her and out of the corner of my eye, I noticed Jay's eyes watching me. Why look at me now? I was so frustrated. I needed to get away from him to clear my head.

Taking Jolene by the hand I said, "Sweetie, I think it's about time for us to go. Give Aunt Callie and Uncle Justin a kiss and we'll head home." I picked up her jacket and watched as she hugged them goodbye. Jay started to put on his coat obviously to follow us home, but I stopped him. "I think we'll be fine by ourselves tonight." He looked puzzled but relieved at the same time. I wrestled Jolene into her Dora the Explorer jacket, gave Callie and Justin my goodbye hugs and wished everyone goodnight. I took Jolene's little hand and was starting to leave when Jay stopped me to give me a peck on the cheek. He bent down in front of Jolene, gave her a squeeze and let us out the front door. I could feel his eyes following me until the door closed behind us. Out in the fresh air, I took a cleansing breath, bundled Jolene into the car and took my wounded heart home.

Chapter 2

A week after Callie's birthday, I started planning her bachelorette party. I know, that seems fast but they decided to get married as soon as possible, and I was forced into action. Planning a wild party for a pregnant friend was a bit of a challenge, inviting her friends was no challenge at all. I hacked into her Facebook account (I figured out her password was her name) and sent messages to her closest friends from college. I invited Mari-Anna and a few other ladies from the Mathewson Group who'd been on her friends list. I invited Callie's neighbor, Mrs. Callahan, and she insisted on providing party favors, so I gave her a list of the guests and left that job to her. I figured we could all use some mini-hand lotions and lip balms. Callie's mom volunteered the use of her husband Tony's new restaurant for the festivities. He insisted on catering, so the only thing I had to do was come up with some party games. I asked my neighbor Maegan if she'd babysit for me that night. Always underfoot, her triplets overheard and were so excited when they found out, they begged to take Jolene to Chuck E. Cheese. Maegan agreed, and I was so appreciative that she'd take Jolene, I paid for all of them to go. I could tell Maegan appreciated it since her husband, Nate, was a long-distance truck driver who was gone a lot so she rarely got out of the apartment.

I'd gotten a hot outfit to wear to the party at a local boutique. I'd found a fitted white dress with cap sleeves and the waist was accessorized by a thin belt accented with little diamonds. When I knocked on the door to pick up the guest of honor, Justin answered and his eyes grew wide. "WOW! Umm, I don't think my fiancée's going out with you looking like that. Give me a minute to let me get ready. I'm going with you guys," he said grabbing his coat.

"Ha, Justin," I said sarcastically. "You seem to forget this is going to be a pretty tame night since you took the party out of my girl." I playfully pushed him out of the way and yelled. "Callie, are you ready?" I heard a muffled reply from their bedroom. Justin led me to the back of the apartment where we found Callie sitting on their bed in her robe, surrounded by several outfits. Justin stayed at the door motioning me

to go in. When she looked up, I saw tears in her eyes.
"What's up? Why are you crying?" I asked sitting
down on the bed and putting my arm around her
shoulders.

She sniffled with big tears dangling from her
eyelashes. "I look like a fat cow in these clothes.
Justin keeps telling me I look sexy, but I know he's only
saying that because he loves me."

I glanced up at Justin who was studying Callie,
shaking his head in disbelief. "She has no idea how
gorgeous she is, Jane. To me, she's the most beautiful
woman alive and the pregnancy has made her even
sexier."

Callie hiccupped, wiping her eyes with the back
of her hand. "See, he's just blatantly lying to me. Isn't
he wonderful?" She whined. "I love him so much."
She threw out her bottom lip in her famous pout.

I could see this was going to be a challenge. I
pulled out my phone and started pulling up my photos.
Callie sniffled, eyeing me suspiciously. I found the
picture I wanted and held the phone up to her face.
"Now, tell me, does this woman look like a fat cow?"

Callie grabbed the phone holding it closer, then further away. "Wait, this is me!" She said before sticking her tongue out at me.

"Yes, this is a picture I took when we went to the park a week ago. You were playing with Jolene, and I couldn't resist taking a picture. Callie, you're gorgeous, from the back you don't even look pregnant," I said pointing out her shapely waist.

"You cheated. You're not supposed to make me feel better." I saw the hint of a smile as she bumped me with her shoulder, then the lip came right back out.

"All right woman, enough of this wallowing, let's get you dressed. Justin...OUT! You don't get to see until she's completely ready." Justin quickly scrambled from the doorway, pulling the door closed. I stood for a moment looking at the different options and then grabbed a beautiful sleeveless top in deep purple which I paired with a pair of black skinny maternity jeans. My finishing touch was a short black jacket. I fished a pair of flats out of her closet and tossed them to her. "This is perfect. Go get your ass beautified. Oh, and get that pout off your face!" Sticking her tongue out again, she scooped up the clothes and headed into the bathroom.

I dashed out of the room in search of Justin. He was hiding out in the kitchen and looked startled when I came flying in. Making sure she couldn't hear I asked, "Has she been like this long?"

Justin paused. "Yes and no. It's like a hormonal rollercoaster. The doctor said it's normal but honestly, I walk a fine line. If I compliment her, she takes it the wrong way and if I don't she throws out that bottom lip and pouts. I can't win."

"Well, you'd better figure something out before you go on your honeymoon. You'll be together for a whole week in a place teeming with half-naked non-pregnant people. I can totally see a meltdown in your hotel room with her bawling her eyes out."

Justin nodded. "Jane, I can't emphasize it enough. I've tried to stay with her as much as possible and show her lots of attention. She's usually such a strong woman but this has changed her whole personality."

I agreed. "I can see it. Just hang in there with her. I was emotional during my pregnancy but not to this extreme. I'm getting the impression she's feeling self-conscious about the weight thing. I'm sure it's due to her mom's emphasis on not gaining weight."

I heard the bedroom door open so we killed the conversation. I quickly grabbed the latest "People" magazine and started thumbing through it while Justin pretended to be digging through the fridge for a snack.

"Ta-da!" Callie said entering the room and spinning in place. I looked up and was so stunned I dropped the magazine. She looked so freaking beautiful. She'd pulled her hair up into a twist, her makeup was flawless and she'd found some gorgeous dangly earrings to match the purple in her shirt. Justin looked up from the fridge, and I swear his eyes almost fell out of his head. He stood staring at her, and I could feel the electricity between them. "Babe, are you sure you've got to go? I don't want you to leave me. You look amazing. Don't go," he pleaded.

Callie giggled. "Justin," she said rolling her eyes, "I won't be gone ALL night." She gave him a suggestive wink. He wrapped her in his arms before giving her a passionate kiss. Whistling softly, I picked up the magazine again immersing myself in the latest on Tim McGraw to give them some privacy.

After several minutes, I heard, "Jane, you can look now." I saw Callie, face flushed, headed to the door.

"It's about time," I said sarcastically as I grabbed my purse. I gave Justin a quick hug and promised I'd take good care of his woman.

We rode to the restaurant in my car and as we turned into the parking lot, we saw several familiar cars. Tony had set us up in the private dining room and he'd had the staff take care of putting up the decorations I'd bought. As we walked to the back of the restaurant, we heard a loud cheer. Obviously, Callie's friends had been sampling the complimentary bar and they were ready to party. Callie's mom was in the corner talking to Mrs. Callahan and her friend Michelle. Everyone came rushing forward to hug Callie and congratulate her. I'd never met her college friends so Callie introduced me to everyone, and I was pleased to find out they were all great ladies. We mingled and enjoyed cocktails until the servers put out the food. The hors d'oeurves were insanely good and we ate until we were stuffed. We'd just placed Callie in the obnoxiously decorated chair of honor, so we could start the party games when I noticed a police officer coming through the door of the private room. He looked around the room and then spoke to someone standing close to the door who pointed to Callie. Crazy thoughts ran through my mind...was there an accident? Was someone hurt? I moved over to stand beside Callie as he approached. "Ma'am." He focused directly on her. "I understand you're Callie Brandon." Callie's eyes were wide as she looked up at me, so I put my hand on her shoulder and gave it a squeeze. She looked back at him and nodded. "I'm Officer Taylor. We've had a noise complaint with regard to your get-together." He motioned around the room at the stunned ladies who now had moved into a tight circle around her.

"I'm sorry?" She stammered. "I don't think we've been loud at all."

"Ma'am, that's not what I've heard." He paused to consult his little black notebook. "In fact, I've heard you've been a very... bad... girl." It took a moment for me to register what he said. Callie's eyes were huge and her mouth fell open as he removed his hat, throwing it to one of the ladies. Music started playing and I saw it was coming from a boom box being held by none other than Mrs. Callahan. As I gaped at her, she winked and started shaking her hips to the music. Oh my God, Mrs. Callahan hired a stripper! The "policeman" was now gyrating to Pitbull's "I Know You Want Me" directly in front of Callie. He slowly untied his tie, slid it from his collar and wrapped it around Callie's neck. By now, all the ladies were enthusiastically whistling and yelling for him to take more off. I got caught up in the fervor and found myself laughing and clapping along with the music. Our hot cop slowly unbuttoned his shirt to reveal a six-pack that was rock hard. Despite being really buff, he had amazing dancing skills. He was rolling his hips suggestively in Callie's face and all she could do was hide behind her hands. Her ears were bright red and even though she was totally embarrassed she was laughing her ass off. He put his foot on the arm of the chair next to Callie and as he unbuckled his patrolman belt he made sure to wiggle his hips suggestively as the belt passed through each loop. He swung the belt around his head like a lasso and then tossed it. Mari-Anna grabbed it in mid-air then held it aloft like a trophy. Giving us a devilish smile, he unbuttoned his pants then slid them down slowly by hooking his thumbs in his waistband to reveal a little of what was underneath and I had to look twice. He had on a pair of boxers decorated with little hearts and as he slid his pants down I could see a message emblazoned across the rear that said "Got a HEART ON for the bride." Cracking up, I poked Callie to make her look. She peeked between her fingers and started laughing. The final note of the song ended with him rolling his abs and making his pecs jump. We gave him a rousing ovation. He blew kisses while taking his bow. Callie was still laughing so hard she had tears streaming down her cheeks. We all thought the show was over but he didn't move. A moment later, I heard Barry White's "Can't Get Enough Of Your Love Baby" and his next routine was starting. This time, he got closer to Callie and was shaking his rock hard glutes in her face. She reached up and smacked him and we all started whistling our approval. He tucked his thumbs into the waistband of his boxers and began to slide them down an inch at a time. My mouth was hanging open by now and I thought, surely he isn't going to go all the way! It was then I saw he had on a pair of tiny briefs. The boxers came all the way off and I saw Callie cover her face again. Mari-Anna started waving some dollar bills and he gyrated her way. He pulled his tiny waistband out to let her slip them in as he danced. Leslie was feverishly fishing in her purse for money as were most of the other ladies. He made his way around the room collecting dollars from the appreciative ladies. Finally, as the song ended, he took his final bow. Walking back over to Callie, he gave her a gentle kiss on the cheek. "I hope you have a great wedding," he said with a wink. Several ladies volunteered to gather his clothes and I swear some slipped him their numbers.

Callie got out of her chair and walked over to me. "Did you do this?" She asked laughing.

"Uh, no. I really think Mrs. Callahan did," I said pointing over to the dancer collecting an envelope from her at the door.

"Oh my God!" Callie said shaking her head, still laughing. "She's a mess."

We were interrupted by Mrs. Callahan, who had now picked up a glass and was clinking it with a spoon to get our attention. "Ladies, I've made up some party favors so find the basket with your name on it. It's my gift to you!" She said winking. I walked over to the table filled with little baskets, each wrapped in cellophane. I checked the tags and came up with Callie's and my own. I peeked through the cellophane and my eyes grew wide. Mrs. Callahan had stocked the basket with everything you would need for a sexy romantic night and I mean everything! I saw Leslie tucking hers into her purse with a huge smile on her face. All the ladies were buzzing about their goodies. They were a huge hit. I had to get everyone settled down to put them into game mode. A big hit was "Pin the Junk on the Hunk" which Mrs. Callahan won much to her delight. We played a couple more then the party started winding down. I saw Callie yawning and although she'd done really well, I could tell it had worn her out. I drove her home, making sure she got safely to the door with her gifts and goodie basket.

Justin met us at the door with a huge grin on his face. "Did she really do it? Did she hire a stripper?"

I looked at him in disbelief. "You knew? Oh my God! Did she tell you?"

Justin was laughing as he took Callie's basket. "Yeah she asked me if I'd mind. I told her, hell no! It was classic!" He suddenly became distracted looking at the contents of the cellophane package. "Hey babe, we can use some of this stuff now!"

Rolling her eyes, Callie pulled me in for a big hug. "That's what he thinks," she whispered in my ear. "I'm exhausted."

"Maybe you can save it for the honeymoon?" I said looking at Justin who was in heaven as he laid everything out on the counter. Then again, probably not, I thought to myself. Giggling, I waved goodnight to them and headed home to investigate my own love basket.

Chapter 3

A month had gone by and during that time, Jay seemed to be avoiding me. We worked in the same office every day, but it was all business. I kept catching him watching me but with work, planning the bachelorette party and the wedding, I didn't have time to approach him about it. He never invited us out to dinner like he had in the past and it bothered me. I missed him. It hurt to be so close yet so far. When Jolene asked why he didn't come over, I realized how much she missed him too. I'd mentioned how awkward it was to Callie and she told me I was being paranoid. I'd been hoping to talk to him outside of the office but the situation never arose, until Callie and Justin's big day.

I remember not long after the proposal, Callie told me that Justin wanted to get married as soon as possible. Being a top Executive Assistant, I'd managed to put together a traditional wedding in record time. I'd found a darling chapel that afforded Callie the view of the mountains she loved so much. Invitations had been sent and I'd arranged the reception to take place nearby for the convenience of the guests. Callie and I had taken Jolene shopping with us for our dresses. I'd expected a day of torture but Jolene surprised me by behaving like a big girl. She loved looking at everything in the store. A nice salesperson, who obviously had children, took Jolene with her to pull dresses to try on. I was amazed when she begged to put on the flower girl dresses and we found one that was a pale lilac with a plum ribbon accented by a big white flower. A frilly slip underneath made her skirt poof and she'd twirled in front of us giggling. I'd found a beautiful satin dress with a plunging neckline in plum, matching the ribbon on Jolene's dress. Callie tried on several dresses until she fell in love with a gorgeous white satin dress with tiny bead pearls embroidered on the cap sleeves and the V-neck bodice. The back of the dress was a deep v shape with a criss cross detail that finished with a long train. The empire waist was accented by a skirt of pleated chiffon that flowed beautifully as she walked. The bridal store had done an awesome job altering it so her expanding belly wouldn't be the focus.

Everything had been on schedule the morning of the wedding until I lost Jolene. She'd been in the room with Callie and I and we'd just pinned on her veil when

I noticed it was really quiet. Not good when you have a four year old. I looked around and saw her dress crumpled on the floor in the corner and no Jolene in sight. "I'll be right back," I said in a panic. I searched the back rooms for my missing kid. I was passing the connecting door to the chapel when I heard a lot of commotion behind it. I cracked it open to see if she happened to be in there. She was. I poked my head in and saw a chapel half full of guests. "Jolene Marie Carter! You'd better put that dress back on!" I hissed. I couldn't believe what I was seeing. She was prancing around in front of the guests in the chapel in just her frilly slip. She stopped, saw me, spun around and ended up running into Jay who was coming in the side door with Justin.

Jay bent down, scooped her up in his arms and asked, "Sweet Pea, are you trying to drive your mom totally nuts?"

I really didn't appreciate the insinuation that I was even partially nuts but I didn't have time to deal with that right now. I walked up to them holding her dress out to her. She buried her head in Jay's shoulder. "Jolene, don't you want to wear the pretty dress and help Aunt Callie get married?" I pleaded.

She peeped one eye at me then buried her face again. Jay whispered to her, "I'll take you to Chuck E. Cheese if you let your mom put your pretty dress back on. Plus, I want to see you look like a beautiful princess."

She leaned back in his arms, looked at him and with her little hand, rubbed his cheek. "I will for you. I've missed you." I just about lost it. That had to be the sweetest thing I'd ever seen.

Jay eyes locked on mine, he smiled and handed me my mischievous little one. "I think she's ready." It was the first time I'd really seen him smile since the birthday party.

Jolene looked at me. "Mama, I'm sorry. I wanted to play." I looked into those big blue eyes and couldn't be angry with her.

"I know, baby. Let's finish getting you dressed. Aunt Callie's waiting to marry Uncle Justin. Don't you want them to get married?" I asked, walking her to the dressing room in the back of the church. "I've got something pretty for you to wear in your hair and you get to carry a basket. I'll even let you throw things on the floor."

Her eyes lit up as she started clapping. Amazing how you could offer my child a free pass to throw things and she's all in. We walked back into the dressing room and at the door I had to stop and stare. Callie was absolutely glowing. She was making the last minute adjustments to her veil with her mom's help and I saw her rolling her eyes. Yep, her mom was driving her insane. Despite the eye-rolling, she was breathtaking and I had to blink back tears.

"Aunt Callie!" Jolene squealed. "You look pretty!" Callie looked down to see her yanking on her skirt. "I want to put my dress on, Mama. I want to be a princess."

Callie laughed. "Um, so what happened?"

"Oh gosh, let's see. She was in front of the early guests doing her best Britney impression. She's apparently the warm-up act for the wedding," I said laughing.

Jolene looked up at me with a puzzled look. "Who's Britney?"

I looked down at my precious child and did what any good mom would. "Nobody you need to know. Let's get you back in your dress." I slipped it over her head, pinned a circle of flowers in her hair and handed her a basket full of rose petals. "Sweetie, there are flower petals in here. You can throw them down on the floor when we walk into the church, ok?" She nodded smiling, and I thought to myself how much she looked like a little angel. She was absolutely adorable. I took a last minute glance in the mirror to make sure I was presentable, and then I grabbed Callie's flowers and my own. Callie's veil was voluminous, so I scooped it up in my arms to make sure she got out of the room without dragging a piece of furniture with her.

"Hey, have you seen Justin?" She asked biting her bottom lip nervously.

"Um," I hesitated. "I think I saw him climbing out the back window a little while ago," I said with a frown.

Callie chuckled. "Funny. You're such a liar. I love you for making me laugh." I tried to keep a straight face, but I couldn't. She gave me air kisses before making her way to the door where Tony was standing. Her mom walked up, fluffing her veil one more time and I saw Callie mouth, 'Really?' I moved Jolene to the door and gave her a gentle push to send her down to where Justin and his best man, his dad Joe, were standing. All eyes were on her as she started walking with a huge smile on her face but after taking just two steps, she stopped and dumped the entire basket on the floor. My mouth fell open as I watched my angel then skip down the aisle. The entire church erupted in giggles watching her run to the pew where Jay was sitting and plop herself down next to him. Okay, that would've been a good one for the funny video show. Recovering my composure, I took my place at the door glancing back at Callie and I gave her a smile. She winked, stuck her tongue out then pulled down her veil. Classy. I stepped in rhythm with the music and started toward the front of the church. I looked around as I made my way forward, recognizing smiling faces along the way. I saw Mrs. Callahan with a really handsome younger man. As I got closer, I recognized him as "Officer Taylor" from the party. I bit the inside of my cheek to stop myself from laughing. Not bad, Mrs. C., not bad. She winked and squeezed his knee as I passed. In the next pew, Jay sat with a fixed smile on his face but his face seemed troubled. Just as I passed, Jolene yelled out, "That's my mama!" at the top of her lungs. Cheeks flaming, I moved to the front on the bride's side. Justin looked over at me and grinned. I shrugged my shoulders returning the grin. Kids, gotta love 'em.

At that moment, a hush came over the chapel as the music changed to signal the bride's entrance. I glanced over at Justin and saw his eyes riveted to her face. Callie was escorted down the aisle by both her mom and dad. I swear there wasn't a dry eye in the place. Joe patted his hand on Justin's shoulder to comfort him. His mom sat in the front row dabbing her eyes with a tissue.

Callie glided down the aisle, her eyes locked on Justin's. I glanced at Jay and caught his eye but he quickly looked back to Callie. My feelings were taking a beating. Callie reached Justin, took his hand and joined him in front of the minister. She handed me her bouquet and turned to look into the eyes of the man she loved. Justin was in my direct line of sight, and I could see his eyes were brimming with tears. Feeling a lump rise in my throat, I swallowed hard to keep it from turning into a sob. Thinking ahead, I'd tucked a tissue into my bouquet. I discreetly dabbed the tears that ran down my cheeks.

The minister began the service and as I watched my best friend marry her true love, I found myself smiling on the outside, but I felt that twinge of sadness hit me again. This was what I'd always dreamed of. In reality, I'd turned out exactly the way my parents predicted barefoot, pregnant and a single mom to top it off. My thoughts were interrupted by Callie gesturing for the ring. I'd put it on my thumb for safekeeping. I slid it off and handed it to her. She faced Justin and placed the ring on his finger as she said her vows to love honor and cherish. Justin promised the same and placed her ring on her finger. A few final words from the minister, a prayer and they were officially Mr. and Mrs. Justin Brisson. The kiss was a little more R rated than PG, and I quickly glanced over to see if Jolene was watching. No, she was playing a game on Jay's phone, thank goodness. The guests erupted in applause as Callie and Justin made their way out of the chapel to get pictures taken in a local park with the mountains as their backdrop. Jay stayed around until the pictures with the entire wedding party were taken, and then volunteered to take Jolene over to the reception for me since she wasn't needed. We made quick work of the rest of the shots and made our way over to the reception venue. I'd booked a local community center for the festivities and when I walked in, I was thrilled. It was absolutely stunning. A local party planner had set it up. I was struck by the fairy lights draped through tulle flowing from the ceiling and the candlelit tables surrounding the dance floor. Music was being provided by a DJ who was set up on a stage in the corner. Everyone was milling around waiting for the happy couple to make their entrance. I found Jolene sitting at the kids' table eating some chicken fingers. I was wiping her mouth with a napkin when I felt someone grasp my arm. Turning, I found Jay standing right next to me.

"You look stunning, Jane," he said softly rubbing my arm with the back of his hand. I opened my mouth to respond when I heard the DJ announce the arrival of the happy couple. We stood side by side watching them move through the room shaking hands and getting hugs from well-wishers. I felt Jay's hand move to my lower back, and I held my breath. I had to admit the warmth of his hand felt so wonderful.

The first song of the evening began and the DJ announced Justin was dedicating the song to his beautiful bride. All eyes were on them as they moved to the center of the room and began to dance. As I heard the first notes of the song I knew I was going to cry. Justin chose "It's Your Love" and since I was a huge fan of Tim McGraw and Faith Hill, I knew he'd chosen the perfect song. As they slowly swayed to the music, I saw Callie whispering in Justin's ear as he softly kissed her hand holding it to his lips. The guests were mesmerized, and I saw several guests dabbing their eyes. Justin spun Callie halfway through the song and ended up behind her, his hands cradling her swelling tummy as she placed her hands on top of his. It was magical. As the song ended Justin spun her back into a passionate kiss. The guests applauded as the DJ announced father/daughter dance. Tony walked out onto the floor, tapped Justin on the shoulder and took Callie's hand. "You Are So Beautiful" by Joe Cocker started to play as he led her around the dance floor. I watched Leslie fighting back tears as she sat at a table nearby. Jay excused himself leaving my side with a hankie in hand to offer it to her to dry her eyes. After they'd danced for a few moments, the DJ invited any other fathers and their daughters to join them. I felt someone brush by me. It was Jolene. She walked up to Jay, looked up and held out her hand. I took a deep breath trying to stop the tears. Jay looked down and with the sweetest smile, he nodded. They walked together to the dance floor, she held his hands, and stood on his feet while they moved in a circle with the music. It was the most precious thing I'd ever seen. I looked across the room and my eyes found Callie's. She was watching them too, fighting back tears as she danced with Tony. I could feel tears streaming down my cheeks as I watched my little girl have her first dance with a man she thought of as a daddy. As the song finished, the DJ blended it into another slow song encouraging a couples dance. I saw Jay and Jolene walking toward me, but they stopped at Leslie's table where they spoke to her for a moment. Jolene jumped onto her lap, pointed at me and together, they were giggling. Before I knew what was happening, Jay was beside me, taking my hand and leading me onto the dance floor. The song was "I Won't Give Up" by Jason Mraz, which I absolutely loved. Jay turned to face me, pulling me into his arms. He placed his hand on the small of my back and pulled me closer until our bodies were pressed tightly together. Wrapping my arms around his neck I laid my head on his shoulder as we moved to the song. He leaned in and whispered in my ear, "I'm so sorry."

I looked up into his deep green eyes. The eyes I'd only seen this close in my dreams for the past month. "What are you sorry for, Jay?" I asked softly.

He hesitated before speaking. "I'm sorry because I've had something going on in my life and I've let it keep me from doing what I dream of every night."

I whispered, "What would that be?" This couldn't be real. It had to be a dream. His mouth captured mine in an instant, and I couldn't help but kiss him back, my fingers threading through his hair. His broad hands spanned my back, and I could feel his warmth against my bare skin. He had me pressed so close to him that I could feel his heart beating with mine. When we finally took a breath, I realized that the guests were applauding.

I looked around with confusion and saw we were in the spotlight and the applause was for us. I flushed from head to toe with embarrassment but he pulled me close and whispered in my ear, "Don't be embarrassed. I'm not. Jane, I need to tell you, I don't want to leave you tonight. You're all I can think about."

I looked up into his beautiful eyes, "Jay as much as I'd love to, I have to think of Jolene. I haven't really even dated because I don't want it to affect her," I said glancing over at my child.

He followed my gaze. "I understand. I think the world of her, but I want you to know... I won't give up on us. I'm not going anywhere." He'd hit the nail on the head. I was afraid of someone leaving us again and hurting Jolene. As I was about to respond, he smiled and kissed my hand before spinning me around. I suddenly realized that the music had gotten more upbeat. The dance floor filled with people as the DJ played "Cupid Shuffle". The people who knew the line dance showed us how to do it. They were so patient and the steps weren't too difficult. Callie and Justin rushed to join in and we all danced and laughed until we were breathless. Jolene, squeezing between Jay and I, did her Britney dance again and we all laughed watching her concentrating on her moves. The night was so much fun and after several hours of dancing, I saw Jolene was running out of steam. My feet were killing me, so I found a chair in a quiet corner and she snuggled in my lap, her arms wrapped around my neck. I could feel her getting drowsy until she finally fell fast asleep. I managed to stand up without waking her and was trying to grab my purse when I felt a familiar hand on the small of my back. "I'll take her, Jane," Jay whispered gently scooping her from my arms. "Go tell Callie and Justin goodnight. I'll meet you at your car." I watched him take her out the door, and then I made my way over to Callie.

"Hey, hun. Jolene fell asleep and I'm taking her home," I said grabbing my shawl that was hanging over a chair.

Callie pulled me in for a hug. "Thank you for everything. This was a perfect wedding and reception and I love you for making it happen for us. I wish you didn't have to leave. I haven't thrown the bouquet yet and it has your name all over it." I heard her voice break.

"I loved doing it for you guys. Come on, don't make me cry. Throw the bouquet but think of me when you do. Who knows, you might change my luck in the man department." Callie didn't want to let go so Justin pried her away only to hug me tightly himself.

"Jane, try to keep Jay straight while we're on our honeymoon. I could definitely see sparks flying on the dance floor tonight," he said with a wink.

"I confess, I asked them to do the spotlight thing," Callie said laughing with a wicked grin. "I couldn't resist. You guys were totally hot!"

My mouth dropped open. "YOU?" I glared at her for a split second but then started laughing too. "I hate to tell you but that was the equivalent of a cold bucket of water."

A guest beckoned Justin with a gift envelope, so he walked away to speak them. Callie moved in close to whisper so no one would overhear. "Jane, that man is totally into you. I don't know what's holding him back but he needs to build a bridge and get over it."

I was dying to tell her what he said. "He told me he wants to be with me." I finally confessed. Her eyes grew wide. "Calm down, Callie. I told him I couldn't because of Jolene."

Callie nodded. "I understand you not wanting to have sleepovers with her there sweetie, if Justin and I weren't leaving for the airport right after the reception, I'd totally be babysitting so you could take him up on that offer."

"Umm...yeah I could see that being the best honeymoon ever," I said laughing. "Don't worry about me. You guys have fun. I'll keep a lid on the firm and try to keep Jay in line. Don't forget to bring me back a cheesy t-shirt."

As I walked out to my car, I saw Jay leaning against the passenger door. "Jolene's asleep again," he said as he reached for my hand to pull me close, so he could give me another soft kiss. His eyes darkened with emotion. "I can't seem to get enough of you," he whispered brushing my hair away so he could nuzzle my neck.

I melted. "Jay, believe me, if the circumstances were different, you wouldn't be leaving tonight. I can promise you that." I snuggled into his embrace, enjoying it for a moment longer and then pulled away. "I need to get this tired little girl home." Jay insisted on following me home since it was so late. Truthfully, I didn't mind because it meant spending a little more time together.

When we got to my apartment, Jay lifted Jolene from my car and rubbing her eyes, she woke up. "Mama, did I miss the flowers?" She said yawning. She'd been waiting for the bouquet toss all evening, bless her heart.

"Yes, baby. Aunt Callie threw them already. It's ok though, you can have my flowers, okay?" She nodded sleepily.

I was unlocking my apartment door when my neighbor's door opened. "Hey Jane! How was the wedding?" I could hear her triplets screaming through the open door. I could only assume she'd come outside for a break from the noise.

"It was great." I glanced at Jay. "Maegan, this is Jay. Jay… Maegan." Maegan got a surprised look on her face then yelled back into the apartment for the kids. The squealing stopped and three blonde heads poked out the door. They were the cutest little girls, Annabelle, Bridget and Cassidy.

"Jolene!" They squealed in unison. Jolene was instantly awake and wriggled from Jay's arms, running to the girls. The squealing was now four times as loud. We all winced covering our ears.

Maegan yelled over the racket. "Hey, why don't y'all pack a little bag for Jolene and she can stay with the girls tonight." I could've sworn she winked. "It's Saturday night, they can stay up and watch the Spongebob marathon."

Jolene broke away from the pack and ran back to me. "Please, Mama? Please? I promise I'll be good."

She'd thrown out that bottom lip, a habit she'd apparently picked up being around her Aunt Callie. I was a sucker for it so I said okay. She dashed away with the girls and as I turned to go into my apartment I saw Jay sporting a smile that was a mile wide. I was excited but nervous at what that smile might mean. I packed Jolene's nightie, toothbrush and Rapunzel doll. Maegan took the bag and yelled back in her apartment. "Jolene, come give your mama goodnight kisses."

She ran back out the door and jumped into my arms. "Night, Mama. Night, Jay. Jay, you still gonna be here in the morning so we can watch cartoons?"

Jay laughed a deep rumbling laugh. "If your mama doesn't mind, I have every intention of being here when you come home, Sweet Pea." I got tingles all over and blushed.

"YAY! I'm sure Mama won't mind. She likes you. I'll see you then." My mouth fell open at what she'd just said. Giggling, she gave us both a kiss and was absorbed into the squealing mob of blonde ringlets. My obviously perceptive neighbor winked and waved goodnight shutting her door.

Chapter 4

I turned back to see Jay leaning against the door frame. His eyes were hooded as he reached his hand out to take mine. He pulled me inside and shut the door, leaning me back against it. Nuzzling my neck he took my breath away. "Do you want me to be here in the morning?" He whispered. He lightly nibbled my earlobe while his hands stroked my arms causing me to shiver. I nodded silently as he backed away sliding his fingers down my arm to catch my hand.

He gently pulled me toward my bedroom where the moonlight spilled in through my window giving my room a soft glow. Releasing my hand, he cupped my face bringing his lips back to mine in a searing kiss. I sighed feeling my body go slack. Grasping his jacket, I slid it from his broad shoulders. He started to back away to shrug it off but I grabbed his tie and pulled him back. I was the aggressor this time, devouring his mouth with mine. He wrapped his hands around me, and I felt his fingers searching for the zipper of my dress before I felt it slowly being lowered. I pulled his tie from its knot and slid it from his collar letting it drop to the floor. He slid his hands under the straps of my silk gown and eased them off of my shoulders one at a time while softly stroking my skin. My dress dropped slowly, pooling around my ankles. Wearing only my satin panties and heels, I felt so sexy. He pressed my chest to his, holding me with his strong hands, stroking his fingers up and down my spine. Our eyes were locked together, our lips just inches apart. He laid me down on the bed and I stretched my arms over my head, arching my back. He slid his hand down my leg to ease my stiletto off, and then softly kissed the arch of my foot.

"I love you in these sexy heels." He murmured. He removed the other one in the same seductive manner. His eyes never left mine as he slowly unbuttoned his shirt exposing his muscled chest. He slowly eased the shirt off showing me his amazing body and I realized he was giving me my very own strip tease. He unbuckled his belt, slid it from the loops and tossed it to the side. I was practically purring as he slipped his pants off, laying them on the chair. My heart was pounding as I realized this was really happening. I saw him hesitate and knew exactly what he was thinking. Thank goodness for Mrs. Callahan's party basket! I gestured to my nightstand with a wink, where my basket sat holding an array of treasures. He quickly found what he was looking for and joined me on the bed kissing me gently, then more intensely. I clutched his shoulders and found my nails digging into his skin. I responded to his kiss fervently. He slid my panties off, dropping them beside the bed. His body covered mine as he slid his hand down my leg to grasp the back of my thigh pulling me closer to him.

His mouth moved to my neck and he groaned. "Baby, you taste so sweet." He lightly bit my collarbone and I felt a shiver down to my toes. We explored each other, touching and caressing tenderly. When the time was right, our bodies aligned and I closed my eyes letting desire wash over me. As we moved together, I opened my eyes to see his gaze burning with passion. I held him tightly, and as my body tensed, he held me with his strong hands. His mouth was softly caressing mine and a moan escaped my lips. He held the kiss until we cried out together. Both panting and trembling, we lay together until our heartbeats slowed. He kissed my dampened forehead and moved to lie beside me. Wrapping me in his arms, he held me close, my back to his chest. The combination of his warm breath on my neck and his strong arms wrapped around me made me drowsy and I was soon fast asleep.

The next morning, I woke to find the warmth of his arm draped across my bare skin. Feeling me move, he stirred and kissed the back of my shoulder. "Good morning," he said his voice gravelly from sleep. I stretched and turned my head to say good morning to him as well but found a passionate kiss instead. He had scruff on his face and it tickled me as we kissed. I'd always seen him freshly shaven so this look was rugged and very sexy. I finally pulled away to catch my breath and as I glanced over his shoulder at the clock, I suddenly realized that Jolene would probably be home any minute.

"Jay, we need to get up," I said trying to get out of bed. He tightened his grip on me and I had to struggle to get him to let go. Laughing, I finally broke free as he groaned facedown into the pillow. I stood by the bed and swatted him on his absolutely perfect behind. "I don't think Jolene needs to see you in my bed, or in the same clothes you had on last night." I went into my drawer and found an oversized sweatshirt that had been Tyler's. It had been the only thing he'd forgotten to take and I'd kept it as a sleep shirt. Jay rolled over to sit on the side of the bed. He looked at the shirt as I handed it to him and made a face.

"If this was Tyler's, I don't want to wear it. I don't want anything near me that belonged to that scumbag." He growled. He stood, scooped up his clothes and took them to the bathroom. As he shut the door I realized that he was right. I rummaged through my closet and found a flannel shirt I'd found at a thrift store that I used for painting. As he came out of the bathroom, I handed it to him. He looked at me with eyebrows raised and I cleared it up right away. "This is mine... only mine." Nodding with a smile, he slipped the shirt on and was buttoning it just as I heard the doorbell ring. Opening the door, I saw Maegan with Jolene.

"I hope you don't mind, she wanted to come home," she said looking over my shoulder. "I told her I thought your friend Jay might've come over early for breakfast this morning." She winked as she said the last part. Jay came up behind me to rest his chin on my shoulder.

"JAY!" Jolene squealed. "You came over! We can watch cartoons and we can have a tea party and we can play Barbies…" Jay started laughing as she grabbed his hand. She was talking a mile a minute as they walked back into the apartment.

Maegan grinned and lightly punched my arm. "Had a good night, did we?" She waggled her eyebrows.

Making sure we were alone, I whispered, "Try mind blowing." I watched her mouth fall open and as I turned to go inside I said over my shoulder, "Have a great day, Maegan." I winked as I shut the door.

Inside, I found Jay sitting at the little table in Jolene's room. He was joined by Rapunzel and her favorite teddy bear. She'd arranged her tea set and was "pouring" him a cup of tea. I leaned on the doorjamb watching and found myself fighting back tears. My little girl was so grownup. She looked so serious as she handed the cup to him. Jay accepted his cup graciously and asked her how her evening had been.

"It was good." She began seriously. "Miss Maegan let us stay up til 10:30! And then this morning, Miss Maegan made us chocolate chip pancakes!"

He laughed. "Sounds better than good to me!" Holding the cup and pretending to blow on his tea, he held his pinkie out. He sipped and made a yummy noise. Jolene watched him closely then imitated him. It was so beautiful watching them together.

"I'll be right back," Jolene said starting to get up from the table and saw me standing there. "Mama, can you get some cookies to go with our tea?" She said jumping up and down in front of me. I looked at those precious blue eyes and melted. Nodding, I went to the kitchen, pulled a package of chocolate chip cookies from my special hiding place and carried them back to her bedroom. Teddy bear had now been tossed aside and there was an empty chair for me.

"Mama, Mr. Teddy had to go to a parade. I saved you a seat." Jay grinned as he stood to pull out my chair. He kissed the top of my head as I perched on the tiny chair. I dropped a cookie onto each plate and our hostess poured me a cup of her tea.

"Mama, you have to do it like this," she said, holding her cup with her pinkie out. I held my tiny cup and tried to imitate her causing her to giggle. "Mama, you're so funny." Soon we were all laughing and it struck me, this is what a real family is supposed to be like. We played tea party until Jolene got bored and then she switched her attention to cartoons.

I made Jay and I some scrambled eggs and we all piled on the couch to watch "Dora the Explorer". Jolene claimed the couch on one side of me leaving Jay and myself sitting next to each other. She kept a running commentary on everything that happened and I was so impressed at how she'd picked up words from other languages.

She wriggled and fidgeted next to me and at one point her foot ended up on my shoulder. I glanced at Jay, laughed and shrugged my shoulders. It wasn't long after that, her night with the triplets caught up with her. I heard her snoring. She'd ended up with her head in my lap, arms around my waist, and was now happily snoozing away.

I felt Jay slip his arm around my shoulders and he scooted as close as he could without waking her. I turned to see him smile as he looked at me. He twirled my hair with his finger and watched as it unfurled. Licking his lips, he focused his eyes on my mouth and I

instinctively licked my own. He mouthed, 'I want you.'
I could feel all the passion and desire from the night
before come roaring back. I mouthed, 'I want you too.'
He winked and turned his attention back to the tv
which now had "Yo Gabba Gabba" on. We sat quietly
together for quite a while, waiting for Jolene's nap to
end. Finally, she stirred and Jay took the opportunity to
get up and stretch.

"Girls…I need to run but enjoyed spending time
with you both." He leaned down and gave Jolene a
kiss on her forehead. She mumbled something that
sounded like "I love you" as she turned over on the
couch releasing me from her grip. I took the
opportunity to hop up and walk him out. At the door
he took me into his strong arms and held me tightly
against him. I laid my cheek on his chest while he
rested his chin on the top of my head. We stood like
that for a moment then he pulled back and looked
down into my eyes. "You have the most beautiful blue
eyes," he said softly. "Jolene's a lucky girl to have your
eyes. She's going to be a heartbreaker."

I thought of Tyler for a split second and realized I
didn't want Jay to know how closely she resembled her
father. I liked him believing I had a hand in creating

those beautiful blue eyes. I looked up at him and smiled. "Yes, I'm going to have to lock her up from the boys when she starts school." I hugged him a little tighter. "Jay, I really don't want you to leave but I understand. There's only so much Nickelodeon a person can stand in one day." I laughed.

"Baby, I could watch paint dry with you two. I'd be just as happy staying, but I really need to get some things done before work tomorrow. You're still working for me right? I'm going to have you all day tomorrow?" He said with a gleam in his eye.

"Oh yeah, that's right. You're still my boss. I'll HAVE to see you tomorrow," I said winking.

"I can't wait," he whispered. I completely melted as flashes of the night before made my face flush and he leaned down and kissed me gently. "See you in the morning." He opened the door, walked out, and glancing back he blew me a kiss. I watched him until he was out of sight, sighed and then closed my door.

Chapter 5

I arrived early the next morning to make sure all the appointments for the week were confirmed and the necessary paperwork caught up. I'd also taken extra time with my makeup and hair, wanting to look gorgeous for Jay when he walked in. I'd gotten a text from Callie as soon as I sat down at my desk.

Hey girlfriend, how's it going?

It's all good. How's Jamaica?

Tropical. Out of curiosity, anything interesting happen last night?

Was she psychic? I knew what she was hinting at but really?

Maybe?

Look do you want me to fly back and kick your ass?

I laughed out loud at my mental picture.

A pregnant woman kicking my ass. That could be interesting.

JANE!

All right Jay spent the night.

Literally, seconds later.

EEEEEEP! I'm so happy for you guys!

Thanks. I pray we haven't ruined everything by taking that step.

There was a long pause.

Jane it can only get better. They say down here, don't worry be happy.

I missed her already. I sent her a picture of me waving sporting a goofy smile.

A few minutes later, I got a picture back. It was of her pink toenails splashing in the surf.

Hey I want to see that face not your toes!

You don't want to see a beached whale this early do you?

I sat there dumbfounded. She wasn't serious, was she?

Are you being serious Callie? You are a beautiful woman. Cut out the whale talk ok?

I waited patiently for a response.

Okay. I love you Jane. I'm just feeling fluffy among all the hard bodies today. Forgive me? I'll talk to you again soon.

I love you too and there's nothing to forgive. HUGS!

I heard the front door open as I hit send on the last text. It was Jay. I'd always thought he was drool worthy but this morning I saw something different. He really should've been a model. He'd picked a dark blue suit this morning which he accented with a deep burgundy tie and matching hanky. I'd had the biggest crush on him since that day in Callie's office but now I felt a rush of emotions, possessiveness, pride and honestly, a healthy case of lust. I stood as he came toward me and in one motion he gathered me tightly in his arms and gave me a toe-curling good-morning kiss that almost made me faint. "I missed you," he growled. As he gently let me go, I flopped back dramatically into my chair. I fanned myself with a piece of paper I snatched from my desk. His luscious mouth curled into a smile. He turned and swaggered into his office. I got up to follow him for round two but was stopped by the phone ringing.

"ABC Designs, Jane Carter speaking," I said a little breathlessly.

"Jane? This is Mari-Anna Baker over at Mathewson. I'm glad I caught you. Hey, I need to ask you a question." She paused.

"Um...sure. If this is about Officer Taylor, I think he's taken." I laughed.

She laughed. "No, that's not it. Actually, I know this is going to sound weird and random but...do you have a brother?"

"Well, that is random but no, why?" What a strange question.

"Hmm, that's odd," she said distractedly while mumbling, it sounded like she was scooting papers around. "Where did I put that note?" She paused again. "Okay, here it is, he didn't give his name but left a number."

At the mention of a man claiming to be my brother, I got a sick feeling in my stomach. I didn't like this at all. "Someone claimed they were my brother? Did you speak with him?"

"Actually, no. My secretary, Amber spoke to him. He told her that he was your brother and he needed to get in touch with you right away. He asked if you were in the office and she told him no because she had a weird feeling about him and didn't feel right giving out any information. Now I'm glad she didn't."

I had a feeling I knew who this was but I had to be sure. "May I speak to Amber? I'd like to know what this guy looked like in case I need to be on the lookout for him since he's obviously not a part of my family."

"Sure. Hang on, I'll grab her." She placed me on hold and recorded music played while I waited. I nervously took a paper clip from my desk and straightened it while listening to the instrumental version of "Love Story" by Taylor Swift. I heard Jay's door open behind me and I spun my chair around. He saw I was on the phone so he mouthed, 'Come here when you get free.'

He'd just shut his office door when I heard the phone pick up, "Amber speaking."

"Hey Amber, I need to ask a question, if you don't mind." My bad feeling had intensified and was making me nauseous. "The guy who was asking about me, can you describe him?"

She paused for a moment. "Well, first of all, I didn't tell him anything about you because I remembered Miss Brandon saying something about you not having any family. I didn't want to cause you any drama. He was probably mid to late twenties, sandy brown hair, striking blue eyes. Really nice looking. "

I felt my heart stop. No, no, no. Not now. I felt lightheaded and the room was spinning. I managed to sputter, "Thanks Amber. You did the right thing. If he comes back, please don't tell him anything about me, okay?"

"Umm, sure. Is everything all right?"

"I really don't want to go into it but please, don't tell him anything." I hung up, staring at the phone.

Why now? What did he want? The man who'd dumped me five years ago and who I hadn't heard a word from in all that time.   My first thoughts were of Jolene. I really didn't want her to know he existed. Tyler had walked out on us and I wasn't going to let him waltz back in.   I heard Jay's door open but I couldn't move. He rushed over to kneel in front of me. "Jane, what's wrong? Baby, you look like you've seen a ghost."

I couldn't tell him. This was something I needed to keep to myself until I could figure out what to do.   I looked into those beautiful green eyes and lied. "My favorite aunt passed away."

He gathered me up into his arms and held me. I felt the tears rolling down my cheeks. "I'm so sorry, baby." He held me as my silent tears turned to sobs. I cried until I couldn't cry any more. "Are you going to be okay?" Jay asked trying to dab my cheeks. I realized then he was using his beautiful silk hanky. I looked up at him and shook my head. "You're not going to be okay?" He asked full of concern.

"I'll be okay, it was just a shock. Jay, I'm sorry I blubbered all over your suit and your beautiful hanky," I said, sniffling.

"Your aunt just passed away. Of course you're going to be upset. I don't care about the hanky. I can get it dry-cleaned." He pulled me close again, and I felt wrong for lying.

I dabbed my tears and managed a smile. "Thank you so much. You knew just what I needed." I took a deep breath. "It'll be okay." Quickly composing myself, I pulled away and stepped over to my desk. "Before I forget, you had a call from a...Mr. Davenport bright and early this morning. He said he'd heard good things about your architectural projects and wanted to discuss a possible project with you. I jotted down the basic information and told him you'd get back to him." I handed him the memo slip.

"Ah, I know who you're talking about. I've heard rumors that they've been planning a new bank building in town and several firms are up for the project." He gave me a quick kiss on the cheek. "I'll give him a quick call. You sure you'll be okay?" I nodded yes as he walked away and I slumped down in my chair. Tyler was back, what could he possibly want? I couldn't gather my thoughts here at work. I needed to focus on my job right now. Within a few minutes, Jay called me into his office to go over what Mr. Davenport wanted.

"Jane, are you feeling better?" I nodded. "Okay, I'll need you to pull the First Bank and South Bank building designs. They'll be our example projects. Also, could you pull Callie's Medical Center plans? I think that will show them our general style." I was thankful for the diversion and threw myself into the planning and organizing of everything. Jay didn't have to have the final plans, just a proposal of the firm's vision for the board to consider.

I felt guilty all day because Jay was so compassionate, checking on me constantly. I found out the big meeting was scheduled for Monday morning so we had time to make a PowerPoint presentation and Jay even laid out some preliminary plans based on his conversation with the client. I'd never really worked this closely with him and it amazed me how talented he was. At the end of the day, we were both exhausted and I looked at the time realizing I needed to get Jolene from day care. Jay walked up behind me and began massaging my shoulders. "You want some company tonight? I could bring Chinese."

I closed my eyes and moaned. "I'd love Chinese. I'm too exhausted to cook. Order whatever you like, I love it all."

Brushing my hair aside, he softly kissed the nape of my neck. "Great, I'll call it in now and grab it on the way." We gathered our things and he walked me out to my car. As I was getting in I felt a weird feeling, like someone was watching. I looked around but didn't see anything out of the ordinary. He leaned into my car and gave me a kiss. "Be safe, baby."

I picked up Jolene and told her we'd be having company for dinner. She was so excited and chattered all the way home. We'd just unpacked her drawings from daycare when Jay knocked on the door. As I opened it, I was brushed aside by my wild child. Jolene squealed. "JAY! You brought me food!" Seeing the familiar takeout cartons she asked, "Do you have the cookies?"

Jay laughed, "Yes, I got you the cookies. We'll have to see what your fortune is after we eat." He came in and sat the bags on the table. I started looking at the array of food he'd brought.

"How much do you think we eat?" I said laughing. "Jolene will only nibble on an eggroll."

"Haven't you heard? Chinese food makes the best leftovers." Laughing, he proceeded to open the cartons and I saw orange chicken, shrimp fried rice, beef and broccoli, and several eggrolls. I got some paper plates out and put an eggroll out for Jolene. She'd dug around in the bags and found chopsticks and I watched her carefully try to pick up the eggroll with them. Jay was digging into his orange chicken and realized what she was doing. "Sweet Pea? You need some help?"

She was struggling, refusing to give up. "No, I got it." She chased the eggroll around the plate and I was now laughing so hard, I was crying. She finally took a chopstick and stuck it right through. Triumphantly, she held it up and nibbled on the end dipping it in sweet and sour sauce.

Jay was laughing. "Well, that's one way to do it." He took the other chopstick and speared a piece of chicken. "In fact, this really works great!" He and Jolene started laughing together. Seeing her with Jay brought back the memory of the phone call about

Tyler. Obviously, it showed on my face because they both looked at me with concern.

Jay started to get up. "Jane, are you okay?"

"You ok, Mama?" Jolene said rubbing my arm. "I'm fine. I just had some upsetting news today. It's nothing you need to worry about." I said running a finger through her beautiful curls. She smiled and went back to nibbling on her eggroll. Jay gave me a half-smile. He had to be thinking I was referring to my aunt. I really didn't feel hungry but I sat down and began nibbling on some beef and broccoli. We sat like a family, chatting about our day.   It felt so natural and it helped me forget for at least a little while. After dinner, we all went to the living room and sat curled up on the couch. Jolene took over the end of the couch, leaving Jay and I sitting next to each other again. She grabbed the throw off the arm of the couch and a pillow and snuggled next to me. Jay put his arm around the back of the couch and stretched his legs out. It was so cozy, and I could feel the heat from his body. I felt him twirling my hair again, and I glanced over and smiled. He winked and moved his hand under my hair where he started to massage my neck again. I leaned into him and I could feel the tension of the day slip away as his strong hands worked to relax me. I snuggled closer, resting my hand lightly on his thigh. We sat watching one of Jolene's favorite movies "Finding Nemo". It was actually one of my favorites and I found myself laughing out loud like a kid. I could tell Jay was watching me and he had the biggest smile on his face.

"I love watching you laugh," he whispered, while still gently rubbing the back of my neck. His touch became gentler and I could feel tingles all over. Suddenly, I got kicked in the side. Jolene was asleep and apparently dreaming of taekwondo. Smiling, Jay slowly got up and, wrapping her in the throw, carried her to her room. I made sure Rapunzel was safely next to her as I tucked her in. She barely stirred as I shut off her light and followed Jay to the living room. Suddenly, he spun around and pulled me to him. We were nose to nose and he whispered, "I want you so badly. I can hardly stand it."

Reaching up to run my fingers through his hair, I whispered back, "I want you too. We should snuggle on the couch and make out." I waggled my eyebrows at him and pulled away leading him to the couch. Jay laid down, and I crawled up next to him. I kissed his neck, his ear, finally reaching his luscious mouth. He wrapped one arm around me pulling me closer and slid the other through my hair, cupping the nape of my neck to pull me in for a deeper kiss. We kissed until we were breathless. "That was amazing," I whispered against his lips. Jay's eyes were dark with desire. I knew what was on his mind, but I couldn't bring myself to do that with Jolene in the apartment. I was going to have to find a way to be alone with him again, soon!

"Babe, I know what you're thinking. I'm okay with waiting," he said kissing my forehead. I laid my head on his chest and listened as his wildly beating heart slowed. He ran his fingers gently through my hair as I wrapped my arms around his waist. We lay, legs tangled together and I could feel myself getting drowsy. I closed my eyes, took in a deep breath and was gone.

Chapter 6

I felt a tickling in my ear. Rubbing my ear, I ignored it. Then I heard a giggle. I cracked open one eye to see my daughter standing over me and was suddenly wide awake. Looking beside me, Jay was still sleeping. We were still on the couch and I looked at the clock on the cable box and it read 6 am. "Jay, wake up." I poked him and Jolene giggled. "Jay, we slept all night on the couch. Jolene is here," I said the last part loudly and he jerked awake.

"Mama, you snore," Jolene said still poking me. Jay looked at me and started laughing. Really? My daughter had just found us tangled up on the couch and he was laughing?

"Relax, Jane. We were just sleeping," he whispered. "If you don't make a big deal out of it, she'll be fine."

I looked at Jolene and she was happily watching "Spongebob" oblivious to anything out of the ordinary.

Jay untangled his legs from mine and sat up rubbing his eyes and running his fingers through his hair. He had sexy scruff again this morning and I just wanted to grab him and kiss him. "Do you want some coffee?" I asked as I got up and stretched my back. Giving him a wink, I padded toward the kitchen.

He got the hint and followed me. "I wish I could but I need to run home and grab a shower. I'll see you shortly at the office." Out of Jolene's view, he kissed me tenderly. He walked back to Jolene stopping to give her a kiss on the top of her head. "See you later, Sweet Pea."

I waved my hand in front of her to break her gaze on the tv. "Jolene, I'm going to make you some breakfast. Go get dressed and I'll be in to fix your hair then we'll eat," I said. I saw her get up, eyes still glued to the tv, dragging her doll along behind her. I followed Jay to the door wrapping my arms around him from behind. I gave him a squeeze and laid my head on his back breathing in his masculine scent. He spun around and looking to make sure the coast was clear, gave me a breathtaking kiss. He opened the door and blew me another one and was gone. I shut the door and was heading back to Jolene's room when

I heard a knock at the door. I saw Jay's jacket on the couch so I turned around and yanked it open. "Did you forg—"

My heart stopped.

"Well, someone looks surprised." Tyler had his hand leaning against the door frame. "Did you think I was the guy that just came out of here in the same clothes he had on last night?" He said smirking.

I stepped out the door pulling it behind me. "Tyler, that's none of your business," I said keeping my voice low. "You gave up the right to know anything in my life five years ago," I said, my voice trembling.

"I want to see my kid, Jane," he said trying to look around me through the crack in the door. I was thankful Jolene was a good girl and would stay in her room until I came to get her. "I have a right to see my own flesh and blood."

That pissed me off. "You don't even know what you have, Tyler because you left me and MY child because you didn't want to be trapped by a kid. Well, you can go on and leave us alone."

His expression changed, softened. He leaned closer. "Jane, I'm sorry. I didn't know how to do this and I'm getting you mad. That wasn't my intention. Seeing that guy this morning rubbed me the wrong way. I want to talk to you. I want to come back, to show you I've changed. I need you and our baby in my life." He looked me up and down. "You look so beautiful. I've missed you so much." He moved to touch my cheek, and I took a step back.

I felt tears welling up. I took a deep breath. "Tyler, you walked out. You dumped me. Now you want me to take you back? How does that work? Am I supposed to forget raising my child alone?" I took another breath and blew it out trying to stop myself from crying. I didn't want him to see me break down.

"Baby, look at me and tell me you don't love me anymore. You promised you'd love me forever." He reached out again to touch me.

I flinched and backed up another step. "Don't call me baby. You made promises too, Tyler. You promised a lot of things and then you broke every promise. Just leave." I started to close the door.

He put his hand on the door to block it. "I'll leave today but I'll be back. I want my kid. I want you." He turned to leave. "Tell pretty boy he's going to have some competition."

I shut the door and locked it. I leaned against it and put my head in my hands wanting to cry. "Mama? You ok?" Jolene came to her bedroom door, her eyes wide.

I wiped my eyes. "Yes, baby. I'm ok. I just got something in my eye." I started to walk to her room and stopped dead in my tracks. Something Tyler said hit me like a brick. He'd seen Jay last night. He knew he'd spent the night. Had he been watching my apartment? He'd obviously not seen Jolene and I thanked God he hadn't. I shivered thinking about the weird feeling I'd had in the parking lot at work. He'd probably staked out the firms in the area and finally found me. Why now? What was Tyler up to? I needed to talk to Callie, but she was still honeymooning, and I didn't want to upset her. She hated Tyler for what he did to Jolene and me, and I didn't want her flying back to defend us.

With trembling hands, I managed to get Jolene's bag packed for daycare and loaded her in the car. I kept looking around to make sure nobody was lurking nearby but didn't see anything suspicious. I dropped her off and warned the staff not to let anyone take her but me. I felt the need to cover my bases, just in case. I drove to work and walked in the office looking over my shoulder. I was just setting my things down at my desk when someone walked in startling me. It was a floral delivery person with a huge bouquet of orange roses. "Jane Carter?" He said holding out his clipboard. Smiling, I nodded, signing my name. Jay was so thoughtful. "Enjoy," he said walking back out. I had pulled the card out of the envelope when Jay walked in. I gave him my biggest smile but my smile quickly faded when I saw the confused expression on his face. It suddenly hit me that these weren't from him. I still had the card in my hand, so I discreetly slid it into my pocket without him noticing.

"Beautiful," he said touching one of the roses.

"They're from a friend. The flowers are to cheer me up because of my aunt." I lied quickly.

"Well, they're really nice. Is there going to be a service for your aunt? Would you mind if I sent flowers?" He said giving me a quick kiss. Before I could speak he said, "Hey, Jolene wasn't too upset about me being there this morning, was she?" He grabbed his mail and headed into his office.

I followed behind him. "First of all, there won't be a service so you don't need to send any flowers. Secondly, Jolene wasn't upset at all. She actually talked about you the whole way to daycare. She wanted to know if you were bringing her Chinese again tonight."

Laughing, he pulled me into his arms. "I'd love to bring her Chinese again, but only if I get to sleep over." He waggled his eyebrows and puckered his lips.

I gave him a quick kiss. "Jay, you're a mess," I said giggling as he pulled me tightly to him.

His look turned serious. "I mean it, Jane. I want to spend the night with you again and I want to wake up with you in my arms." He nuzzled and kissed the side of my neck. My body went limp in his embrace and his hands grasped my hips pulling me in close. I threw my arms around his neck.

"I want that more than anything. I don't want to rush this and risk her getting hurt. If you're willing to take this slowly, we can make this easier for her and for us." I kissed him softly.

"I'm willing, but I'm still going to be taking every opportunity to spend time alone with you," he said letting me go with a pat on the rear. I turned to go back to my desk when I heard him say, "Hey, you dropped something." I stopped and turned back to see him picking up the florist card. Oh crap. He started to hand it to me, then stopped. I could see him reading the card. His eyes came up to meet mine.

"Jane, is there something you want to tell me?" He said his voice serious.

"Jay, I…" I started to explain but he stopped me.

He read the card aloud. "*I will get you back…I still love you. Tyler*" Is this THE Tyler? The deadbeat dad who walked out of your life four years ago? What in the hell is he doing sending you flowers? Jane, why did you lie about it just now?"

I stammered. "I don't know why I lied. He's back in town and…he…um…he came by my apartment this morning."

"He WHAT? How does he even know where you are? Have you been in touch with him?" His voice trembled with anger.

"No. I haven't been in touch with him. He apparently figured out where I work and he followed me home. He saw you leave this morning. He made a comment about you being in the same clothes from the night before. Obviously, he's been watching me. He came to my door right after you left." I started to feel tears welling up.

His eyes narrowed. "Did he see Jolene? Please tell me he didn't."

"He didn't. She was in her bedroom and never heard a thing."

He growled. "What did he want?"

I took a deep breath. "He said he wanted to see his kid. I told him he had no right to know anything about my life. I told him to leave us alone."

"And?" Jay said, his jaw tightening.

"And...he said he was sorry. He said he wanted me and his baby back in his life. He reminded me I'd promised to love him forever and that I'd broken my promise. I told him he'd been the one to break his promise to me and I told him again to leave." I heard my voice break at the end.

"Did he leave? Did he say anything else?" He grated.

"Yes…he left." I hesitated.

"Jane, what did he say?" He now was standing in front of me holding my shoulders. I couldn't look him in the eye. I hesitated. "Tell me. I need to know everything."

"He said to tell you that you'd be having some competition." I didn't mention the pretty boy reference. The situation was already tense and that would have pushed him over the edge.

He let go of me and paced back and forth. He started muttering, "He has no right. He walked out." He had a distant hurt look in his eyes.

I started to freak out. "Jay, he's not coming back into my life. I told him that!" I shouted.   He still kept pacing. I stood in front of him putting my hands on his chest to stop him. He finally looked at me and I saw such sadness. I grabbed him and held on tight. He wrapped his arms around me and buried his face in my hair. "I told him to go away," I whispered. I pulled him to arm's length and looked into those gorgeous green eyes. "I want to be with you."

He cupped my face with his hands and I held my breath as he brought his lips to mine gently at first. They were soft kisses until he slanted his mouth on mine and pulled me close, wrapping his arms around me. Suddenly, I heard the phone ringing. I started to pull away but he kept me for just a moment longer. I stumbled to the phone on wobbly legs and breathlessly answered. "ABC Designs, Jane Carter speaking."

There was silence. I said my greeting again. Another moment of silence and just as I was going to hang up, I heard him. "Jane, don't hang up." I felt sick to my stomach. I looked around to see Jay sitting at his desk with his head in his hands. "I need to talk to you. I want to see you and sort this out."

"Tyler, there's nothing to talk about," I hissed into the phone. "Leave me the hell alone."

"Baby, I know you miss me. I could see it in your eyes this morning. I had to send you those roses to let you know how I feel. The lady at the flower shop suggested sending that color when I told her our story."

"I don't know what you think you saw in my eyes but it was shock and surprise. As far as flowers go, I have no idea what the color means and I don't care. I need you to move on, Tyler. You gave up on me and if you think four years later you can waltz in like nothing happened, you're an even bigger fool." I tried to keep my voice low so Jay wouldn't hear me. I peered over my shoulder and saw him turn on his computer.

Tyler's voice dropped real low. "I know you still want me. I'll stay away from the kid until you're willing to let me back into your life. I think about you all the time. I was young and stupid and the thought of a kid scared the hell out of me. I know now that it was wrong and I want to make it up to you."

I listened in silence. I knew the real reason he left. He'd loved his partying more than me, and being a father would have just slowed him down.

"Jane, you still there? I just want to meet my...ah hell...I don't even know. I've told everyone I have a kid and they say "boy or girl?" and I can't say. Don't you want our kid to know me? They will probably hate you later in life for keeping us apart."

I flinched. He was making some sense. I wasn't giving my daughter the option. "Tyler, let me think about it," I finally said.

"Oh babe, you won't regret this. I promise. I'm staying at a hotel on the edge of town. I'll give you my cell number in case you want to reach me." He gave me the number and I jotted it down and slipped it in my purse.

"Tyler, I never said this was a sure thing. I'll think about it."

"Well, think about it and call me. I still love you, Jane. I always have, I just got lost for a while," he said softly.

I felt my heart break. Did I still have feelings for him? Despite all the crap he'd put me through, I still cared. Damn him, why now? I had to get off the phone before I broke completely. "Goodbye, Tyler," I said trying to keep my voice steady.

As he hung up I heard him say one last time. "I love you, babe."

Chapter 7

Jay came over to the apartment every evening that week and never brought up Tyler again. He asked if he could stay over, on the couch of course, and we fell asleep in each other's arms every night. Being with Jay all the time left me no chance to call Tyler. I knew it was a bad idea to call him but in my heart I knew he wasn't going to just go away. I needed to talk to Callie and get her advice. Jay and I stayed busy working on the presentation for Mr. Davenport and I loved every minute of it. Jay had me working on every part of the plans and it made me feel important. Jay was scheduled to present it Monday morning to the board, so we went over every detail making sure it was perfect. Callie and Justin came home from Jamaica Friday night, and I couldn't wait to talk to her. We had so much to catch up on. She called me as soon as she landed, and we made plans to take Jolene to Carrier Park Saturday morning, so I could talk to her in private.

It was a beautiful morning, mild for April, and we met at the playground. I let Jolene play on the slide and swings while we sat on the bench nearby to watch her. Callie looked awesome. She had a healthy glow and her bump had gotten visibly bigger while she was away. As soon as we sat down, the interrogation began.

"So, tell me EVERYTHING!" She said excitedly.

"Well, Jay and I went back to my place after your reception and my neighbor worked things out for us to be alone together by taking Jolene for the night. He and I have been inseparable since you left and Jolene loves him to pieces. I could totally see myself falling in love with him," I said watching Jolene playing in the children's castle. She'd found a friend and they were climbing on the baby slide. I watched closely to make sure she didn't go too high but, like me, she was afraid of heights so she stayed pretty close to the ground.

"Excuse me?" Callie said, eyebrows raised. "Could fall in love? I thought you were already there."

"Well, there's a hitch. Tyler's back," I said wincing, waiting for her to yell. I wasn't disappointed.

"WHAT THE HE—?" She stopped short realizing the kids were so close. She hissed instead. "What the hell? Jane, please tell me you're joking." She'd now grabbed me by the arm.

"I'm not joking. I wish I was. He showed up at my apartment one morning right after Jay left. I managed to get him to leave, but not before he proclaimed his love and gave me an apology for leaving." I risked glancing at Callie and could see she was steaming.

"And? I'm sure that isn't the end of the story, is it?" She asked between clenched teeth.

I sighed. "No, of course not. That same day, he sent me a dozen orange roses to the office. Jay saw the bouquet, so I tried to hide the card and lie about who they were from." Callie's mouth was hanging open.

"I go away for a week and all hell breaks loose! First of all, do you know what orange roses mean?" She said shaking her head and rolling her eyes.

"No, why? Is it bad?" I felt stupid for not looking it up.

"Oh my God, really? Orange roses mean romance. He wants to get back in your pants!" Callie was livid. "Secondly, why in the hell did you lie to Jay? He's been so good to you. He deserves better than that."

"I am just a dumbass. I know Jay deserves better and that's why I'm trying to protect him because, right now, I don't know how to feel about the whole situation. I doubt Tyler wants back in my pants, anyway." I scoffed. "He said he wants to see his child and that he still cares about me," I said somewhat defensively but realizing how dumb that sounded as I said it. He'd all but said he still wanted me. I just didn't want to acknowledge it.

"Oh crap, he's getting to you, isn't he? He walked out, left you pregnant and alone in a strange town and never once looked back until now. I'm sorry, but as your best friend, I have to tell you in my book that is strike three." Callie looked over at Jolene sitting on the bottom of the slide. "Jane, that child needs a stable man in her life not some loser. He'll probably get bored with the whole daddy thing, leave and break her heart in the end."

I sat there looking at my child. I finally said with a shaky breath, "But I don't want her to hate me one day." I felt tears welling up. "She needs to know the truth."

"Oh my God, will you listen to yourself? She's four years old. She's not suffering without Tyler. He was a freaking sperm donor for God's sake. He gave up the right to be her dad the minute he walked out that door." Callie suddenly placed her hand on her stomach. "Oh crap that hurt."

"What's up? Are you okay? Do I need to get you to the hospital?" I asked anxiously.

Callie shook her head. "No, I think it was just Braxton-Hicks. I've been having them on and off for a week or so. I almost didn't go to Jamaica because of it but my doctor said it would be ok. It's easing off now."

"I'm sorry I upset you, Callie," I said putting my arm around her. "This has been weighing on my mind and I hated lying to Jay about it. He is such a great guy and the sex was awesome. Too bad it was only once." Callie turned and grabbed my cheeks, smooshing my face. "Jane, listen to me. Jay is totally in love with you and if you screw this up, I swear I'll disown you as my best friend. Capiche?"

I reached up and grabbed her hands and pulled them away so I could speak. "I would never do anything to screw it up. I just don't know what to do about Tyler. I don't feel the same way about him, if that's what you're worried about. It's just that I have this gut feeling that I'm hurting Jolene in the long run."

She shook her head. "No, he's going to hurt and disappoint a little girl who hasn't had to deal with his drama. Your thoughts are jumbled because of your past with Tyler. Let him go, Jane."

"I know you're right. I've just got to think this through. Jolene is who I'm thinking of, not myself." At that moment Jolene ran up breathlessly.

"Mama, did you see me sliding? I met a boy. He's my boyfriend now. His name's Jacob. We're gonna get married." She pointed over to a little boy who was now flirting with another little girl. I saw Jolene's eyes fill with tears and her bottom lip quivered. "Mama, he said he loved me." Tears spilled down her cheeks as she bawled her eyes out. Pulling her into a hug and pulling a tissue from my bag, I rocked her and wiped her eyes.

"Shh, baby. It'll be ok. You'll find another boy to love." As I said those words I saw Callie nod.

"You know Jane, it's ironic you should give that advice to her," she said grinning and elbowing me in the side.

I wanted to tell her to shut up but since I'd drilled it into Jolene's head not to say that, I refrained. "Callie, you'd better watch it. By the way, how did my daughter perfect this pout? Could it be from watching you?" I said starting to laugh.

"She loves her Aunt Callie, don't you?" She said pulling Jolene into a hug. By now, my resilient daughter had dried her eyes and was ready to play again. It was so easy. Callie was right. I did need to move on. I decided not to call Tyler and to just leave it alone.

Callie's phone beeped. "Oh man, it's my mom. I was supposed to call her as soon as we got in, but Justin and I were so wiped from our trip that I didn't even text her. I'm in big trouble." She held out her phone to show me the message.

Cal! R U ALIVE?

I studied the phone message. "Does she always text like that? I don't know how you read it," I said laughing.

"I'd better text her back," Callie said looking thoughtful before responding.

No

I was cracking up. "She's gonna kill you, you know that, right?"

Callie grinned. "I love tormenting her. She's probably sitting there now looking at my text trying to figure out how to yell at me in abbreviated words. I'd better call her."

"Go ahead, Jolene and I will go play on the swings over there." I pointed to the other side of the grassy area. "You stay here and rest." Nodding, she dialed her mom.

Jolene and I walked over to the swings and I was just helping her onto the seat when I got that weird prickly feeling again. I turned and saw Tyler standing right behind me.

"Hello Jane. Imagine running into you here. It's been a long time," he said, glancing at Jolene.

I wanted to scoop her up and run, but played it cool so she wouldn't be alarmed. "Tyler. What are you doing here?" I asked between gritted teeth.

"Oh, I was jogging in the area and happened to see you. And this must be your daughter?" He said taking a deep breath while gazing at her.

Jolene had been looking at him while we were talking and she now spoke up. "Hi, my name's Jolene. What's yours?"

"My name's Tyler. Jolene, that's a pretty name. You're a very pretty girl. I've never seen such blue eyes," he said turning to look at me with those same eyes.

"Tyler, this isn't a good time. I told you I'd call you and we'd talk. I'm not happy about this." I couldn't stop my anger from rising.

"Mama, is Mr. Tyler a friend of yours? Like Jay? Can he come spend the night, and bring Chinese, and watch movies with me too?" She asked happily swinging away.

Tyler's eyes clouded. "So, she knows all about that, huh? I don't think I like that at all."

"It's not what you think," I said defensively. "He falls asleep on the couch."

"But Mama, you do that too," Jolene chimed in. Well, there goes that.

Tyler's expression hardened. "I told you I wanted you back and you said you'd give me a chance. I love you, Jane. I want us to be a family."

Jolene was watching carefully. "Mama, is everything ok?" She jumped off the swing and came to stand beside me.

"Yes, baby. Mr. Tyler was just leaving. I'm sure he has places to go, people to see." I pulled her in close, hugging her protectively.

"What the heck do you think you're doing?" Callie came rushing up putting herself between Tyler and me. Tyler took a step back as Callie took one forward. She had her finger pointed in his face. "She told you she'd call you. You just couldn't wait, could you? Do you realize what damage this could do to Jolene? You are an insensitive bastard!" She quickly turned to Jolene and said, "Don't say that word, okay?" Jolene nodded stepping further behind me. "Tyler Simpson, you have done enough damage today. Get in your car and go wherever you need to go, but stay away from Jane and Jolene."

Tyler took another look Jolene, a longer look at me then turned and walked away. When I saw him get in his car and drive away, I started trembling all over. I felt a single tear roll down my cheek. Jolene was watching me carefully. Callie came over and gave us both a hug. I whispered in her ear, "Thank you so much. He caught me off guard. I didn't know what to do."

"That's what family's for, Jane." She hugged me tighter and I saw tears welling in her eyes as well.

I suddenly realized that we had Jolene pressed between us. "Baby, you ok?" I said kneeling down in front of her.

"Who was that man, Mama? Are you okay? Are you gonna cry? Don't cry, Mama." I scooped her up and hugged her tightly. She leaned back and rubbed my damp cheek with her palm. She kissed me softly on the forehead.

"Baby, Mr. Tyler was a friend of mine a long time ago but we aren't friends anymore. You met him today but he's still a stranger and you know how we act around strangers." She nodded. "You don't need to talk to him unless I'm with you, okay? If he should show up at daycare and try to talk to you, you need to run and tell one of the grownups." She nodded, hugged me tightly around the neck then gave me a big wet kiss on the mouth.

I heard sobbing and looked over to see Callie in tears. "You guys are so beautiful. I hope I can be as good a mom as you are, Jane. You have an amazing child. She is your perfect reflection."

Holding tight to Jolene, I wrapped my free arm around Callie and together, we left the park. As soon as I got back home, I reflected on the meeting with Tyler in the park, and I realized I had to tell Jay. I needed to come clean about the phone call and especially the confrontation today. I decided to tell him everything when he came over that evening. I'd offered to make dinner and he'd said he would be over about six. Six came and went and no Jay. I called him but it went to voicemail. I left a message and since

Jolene was starving I fed her, but I decided to wait for him. About an hour later, I got a text

Hey babe. I'm sick. I took some medicine and fell asleep. I think it's a virus. I've lost my voice.

I texted back.

Oh gosh do you need me to come over?

NO Jolene doesn't need this. I need you to call Callie. She may have to do the presentation Monday if this hasn't cleared up.

I panicked. Callie hadn't been in on any of the plans. How was she going to do the presentation without Jay?

Jay she's going to freak out.

I know. If I can't do it, you'll need to go with her. You know the plans. You'll need to go over it before the meeting just in case so she'll be familiar with it.

OMG I don't know

Jane you can do it!

I'll try. I hope you feel better soon! I miss you!

I miss you more. I'm going to take some more meds and pass out.

I called Callie right away. "Cal, we've got a problem."

"What's up?" She questioned warily. I should probably have started with 'this has nothing to do with Tyler'.

"Jay's sick. He's lost his voice and probably won't be able to do the bank building presentation on Monday morning," I said in a rush.

Silence. "Are you saying I'm going to have to do this?" She started laughing but then stopped when I didn't respond right away. "Jane, are you freaking kidding me?" Her voice rose about three octaves, and I heard Justin ask her if everything was okay. I heard her assure him it wasn't anything Tyler related and he'd sounded relieved. She must have filled him in on the park encounter and that was totally fine with me. The more people that knew about Tyler the better, especially with the latest developments.

I finally answered, "Yes, but I can help you. Callie, I've done the entire project with Jay and I know it backwards and forwards. I'll need to come over tomorrow to go over it with you, but I think we can pull this off." I loved how confident I sounded when inside I was a big bag of mush.

There was a long pause and then a big sigh. "Okay, I trust you. What time can you come over?" She seemed to be calming down.

"I'll ask if Jolene can stay with the neighbor and I'll come over first thing, say nine? If that doesn't work out, I'll have to bring her. Will that be a problem?" I asked.

"Just bring her, Jane. If she gets bored, Justin can entertain her. He's got to learn about taking care of a child sometime. I'm sure it will be fine."

"Okay, you asked for it," I said laughing. "I need to run by the office and grab the plans. Thank goodness the PowerPoint was backed up on my laptop as well as Jay's."

Callie whispered, "Well, you'd better bring a lot of tissues because I'm seriously hormonal and may lose it at any time. Justin is ready to pull his hair out. I am as happy as a pig in slop one minute then down in the dumps two seconds later." She shouted to Justin, "What, babe? Oh I was just saying how great you've been about my mood swings." She whispered again, "I've been driving him bonkers. He had to go out at 1 am for Taco Bell because I had a craving. When he got back, I didn't want it. He ended up eating five tacos so they wouldn't go to waste. He doesn't even like tacos." I heard Justin laughing.

I could totally see that. He and Callie had come over one night for dinner and I had made quesadillas. He made a face and I immediately offered to make something else for him. "I'll be fine," he said smiling. "I'm just not a fan of Mexican food."

He started to put one on his plate when my darling daughter said, "Uncle Justin, you can have some of my skettios. I don't like that food either. Mama lets me have skettios instead." She had her bowl of "skettios" in her hand and we all started laughing. She started giggling too and ended up dropping the bowl dumping it all over the kitchen floor. After cleaning her and the floor, I opened two cans and they enjoyed their skettios together.

I smiled thinking of that night. "Well, Callie, you need to start craving skettios," I said laughing.

She was cracking up and I could hear Justin say, "Is she talking about me? What's she saying?" That made Callie and I laugh even harder.

"Girl, I gotta go. My bladder can't take all this laughing. I'll see you in the morning," Callie said between giggles. I managed to say bye and was still laughing after I hung up. I texted Jay to tell him we were going to work on it tomorrow but didn't hear back. He'd said he was going to pass out so apparently he had. I decided to make him some homemade chicken soup that I could drop by his place the next morning on my way to the office.

After a sleepless night without Jay, I crawled out of bed the next morning expecting to have to drag Jolene out of bed but she was so excited to go to Callie's she'd gotten up and dressed herself. She had picked out a lovely lime green t-shirt pairing it with a bright pink pair of leggings. She didn't stop there with her outfit. She had her Hello Kitty purse and matching shoes to finish it off. I was so impressed that she put it together. I was putting the soup in a container when I realized I really should let Jay know I was coming. I texted him.

You okay?

A few minutes passed.

Yes I think I'll live. No voice yet.

Well I'm on my way. Unlock your door.

Jane you are NOT coming in my house. You could catch it.

I'm not coming in. Just unlock your door.

Okay but I'm not happy about this.

We pulled up in his driveway, and I left Jolene in the car as I dashed to the front door. The door cracked open a little, and I saw Jay in his boxer briefs and socks trying to hide behind the door. When he saw me, he started grinning. I was wearing a mask that I'd had from a few months ago when Jolene had the flu. I winked at him and slid the container of soup in the door. He leaned down to pick it up and the door swung open a little more. Oh my, Jay did look good in those boxer briefs. I couldn't resist and let out a wolf whistle. He slowly stood up and shook his booty for me waggling his eyebrows. I laughed. "Go eat your soup. Get better soon. I don't like sleeping without you." He nodded and put his hand over his heart. He mouthed 'me too.' I blew him a kiss over my shoulder as I ran to the car and he pretended to catch it. He was just too precious.

I climbed back in the car and was barraged by questions. Jolene was wound up this morning. "Is Jay okay, Mama? Did he like your soup? When's he getting better? When will he come over again?"

I turned around to look in the back seat as she finally took a breath. I took the opportunity and jumped in. "Yes, don't know, soon I hope, don't know. How's that?" She sat staring at me eyes wide and then burst into a fit of giggles. I laughed with her as we drove to Callie's. When we got there, Justin met us at the door. Jolene went dashing in squealing for Callie leaving Justin and me standing there. "You know that's the normal noise level with kids, right?" I said patting him on the back. "You are going to have so much fun."

"Thanks for the warning," he said chuckling. "I've heard from some people that you don't hear your own kids screaming, just other people's. Is that true?"

Shaking my head, I said, "No, you'll hear every peep from your child. When your little boy breathes just a little differently, you'll hear it. If he were in a room full of crying babies you'd know him by his cry.

Now, there are some parents who choose to ignore their kids but you'll always hear them."

He led me into the dining room where Callie had set up a makeshift office for us. Jolene was standing in front of Callie staring at her belly. Callie was laughing. "Jolene felt the baby kick." Jolene put her hand back out to touch Callie's tummy jumping back again when she felt a kick. "Junior is active today. He probably knows I'm freaked out about giving the presentation tomorrow."

I rolled my eyes. "When are you going to pick a name? I don't picture this child as a Junior. I think you should choose a really popular name, something like Channing," I said waggling my eyebrows.

"Well, Miss Smarty Pants, since I saw "Magic Mike" I don't think I want my baby's name associated with the hot guy who stripped. We've picked a couple of names but don't want to tell them yet in case we change our minds," Callie said pulling out a chair to sit at the table. I stood staring at her with my mouth open. She laughed. "Jane, you know you'll be the first one to know."

"I hope so or else I'm changing my relationship status on Facebook to *its complicated,*" I said seriously before cracking up with her. I got Jolene's bag and pulled out Rapunzel and her portable DVD player. I set her up on the couch with "Tangled" for the five millionth time. I turned on my laptop pulling up all the files we'd need for the presentation then joined her at the table. "Jay's still got laryngitis. I dropped off some soup for him on the way here," I said getting my iPad ready to take notes.

"Crap. I was hoping you'd say he was miraculously cured," she said looking over the plans I'd printed.

"I wish. I didn't sleep very well at all last night. I miss my couch buddy," I said pouting. Callie looked up from the plans and smiled. "What? Why are you smiling?" I asked, eyebrows raised.

"You are so in love it's pathetic," she said laughing. "Justin said he thinks Jay feels the same way about you."

"Really? Did he say something specific to Justin that would make him think that?" I asked a little too eagerly. Busted. "I mean, I'm just curious."

"Right...right..." Callie drawled. "Just curious, right. Woman, we need to get you some time alone when he gets well. Justin and I will take Jolene for a whole weekend so you can get away because we're awesome like that," she said winking.

The thought of a weekend away with Jay made me blush instantly. "Callie, I would owe you big time." I jumped up and hugged her around the neck. "You know I love you." She pretended to be choking while I hugged her. "Just ruin the moment, crazy woman," I said smacking her on the arm as I sat down. "Let's get some work done."

We went over the presentation, and Callie was very impressed with how well I knew it. I showed her the PowerPoint presentation, and we went over the key points and what made our firm's design unique. Justin was awesome while we worked. He fed Jolene lunch (he'd apparently stocked up on skettios) and made us sandwiches. I was impressed with his skills in the kitchen and made sure to compliment him about it. We worked all day and finally we felt we had it down. Jolene was yawning so I gathered up her things to head home. Callie and I made plans to meet an hour before the meeting at Starbucks to go over any last minute details. I hugged Justin and thanked him for being so great with Jolene. "Jane, it was my pleasure. I hope our boy turns out as wonderful as she is."

Callie hugged my neck. "I'll see you in the morning. Get some sleep. I love you, Sis."

After Jolene and I got home, I texted Jay to tell him goodnight.

Sweet dreams. Hope you're feeling better.

He responded pretty quickly.

How did it go?

I think we'll be okay. I'll let you know after the meeting.

I'll be waiting to hear. I miss you babe.

I sighed. He made my heart melt.

I miss you too. I can't sleep.

Funny, I was going to say the same thing.

I needed to tell him about Tyler and wanted to tell him about Callie's offer to babysit but figured it could wait, for now. I got Jolene ready for bed and tucked her in. I went into my bathroom, washed my face, threw my pjs on and fell into bed. I tossed and turned for the second night in a row and lay there thinking about Jay.

Chapter 8

The next morning, I dropped Jolene at daycare and headed to Starbucks. Callie, who was already there, had ordered a yogurt parfait and water. I ordered a Carmel Frappuccino, because I desperately needed some caffeine and a raspberry scone, just because. I joined her at the table.

"How're you feeling this morning, Cal?" I asked setting my drink down. I had my iPad ready in case she'd come up with any new ideas.

"I'm good. I feel pretty confident especially with your coaching. You've worked so hard to make this work. I couldn't be prouder." She put her hand on my arm and squeezed. "If I...wait, when we pull this off, I'm taking you on a shopping spree as a thank you."

"Aww, Cal, you don't have to do that. I have lots of clothes already," I said laughing. I took a sip from my coffee. She took in my modest business blazer and matching skirt.

"You have clothes but I'm not talking about business clothes. I'm talking about a wardrobe from Victoria's Secret. I know you need to spice up your lingerie drawer and I'm going to make that happen," she said winking at me. I almost spit my coffee out.

"Oh my God, Cal. Are you trying to kill me this morning?" I gasped as I coughed.

"No way. You and Jay need to have that getaway weekend and I WILL make sure that happens. I know it's something you really need and want. Plus, I just love you, that's all."

I nodded smiling. "It would be awesome to just have some real one on one time. Oh my God, that sounded dirty.." I giggled. She just shook her head and laughed.

We finished looking over everything and felt really confident. I helped Callie get her bags, and we drove over to the Davenport offices in my car for convenience. As we waited for the elevator, I could feel my palms beginning to sweat. I put on a forced smile for Callie but inside, I felt so sick. This was really important for the firm, so I wanted it to be perfect. I got out my phone to turn it off for the meeting and saw I had a text.

Good luck. I'm with you in spirit. I'm feeling much better today.

I quickly replied.

Glad to hear. Will let you know how the meeting goes.

I shut off my phone and threw it back into my purse. Callie and I stopped in front of a huge reception desk where a young woman sat with her headset on.

"May I help you?" She asked glancing up while typing on her computer.

"Callie Brisson and Jane Carter to see Mr. Davenport," Callie said handing her the company business card.

"We were expecting Jay Anderson. Is there a problem?" She asked reaching over to the fax machine to grab a sheet that had just come in.

Callie spoke up. "Jay is suffering from an unfortunate case of laryngitis. I'm his partner and am very familiar with the project. I'm prepared to present it this morning as expected."

"Okay, you can have a seat over in the waiting area and Mr. Davenport's secretary will come out for you when they're ready." We sat down and had only been waiting for a few minutes when a drop-dead gorgeous blond man walked to the reception desk. Callie and I looked at each other giving the unspoken OMG look and then were startled when he came over to us.

"Mrs. Brisson, Miss Carter? I'm Tristan O'Neal, Mr. Davenport's personal assistant."

We nodded, and I noticed my mouth was hanging open, so I snapped it shut and grinned. Callie was poking me with her elbow as we followed him down the hallway. I noticed that as we passed each office, the employee inside, whether male or female, checked him out as he walked by. He was wearing a very well-tailored gray suit which showed his very muscular physique. He stopped at the door and we almost bumped into him. We scrambled to compose ourselves and put on our biggest smiles. He turned and winked. "Ladies, after you." He opened the double doors and ushered us into the conference room. An older man I assumed was Mr. Davenport stood as we entered and gestured us inside. He walked over to Callie, shook her hand and then extended his hand to me as well. I shook his hand firmly hoping he wouldn't notice my sweaty palm. I heard Tristan say my name and I turned to see he'd pulled my chair out for me. I sat and watched as he did the same for Callie. Mr. Davenport went back to the head of the table to sit in a large executive chair.

"Mrs. Brisson, Miss Carter. My receptionist informed me that Mr. Anderson isn't well. I hope it's not serious." He seemed genuinely concerned so I spoke.

"He appears to have caught a virus but when we went over the last minute details this morning. He seemed to be on the mend," I said as Callie nodded.

"Well, we'll get this meeting started as soon as the other firm's representatives arrive. I hope you don't mind but in the interest of time, we scheduled a presentation from Grayson and Chase also. We will listen to both proposals and then make our decision."

The phone in the corner beeped and Tristan answered. After speaking for a moment, he walked to

Mr. Davenport and whispered in his ear. Mr. Davenport nodded and Tristan walked back out of the conference room. Callie and I pulled out our laptops and paperwork. We opened all the files we'd need and had it ready to present. An adjoining door opened and an elderly gentleman entered. He walked stiffly over to a chair and slowly sat. A couple of minutes later, a middle-aged woman entered carrying an iPad. She sat next to the older man and they whispered to each other. I could feel my leg jiggling with nerves and I consciously had to stop it from banging the table. Callie pinched me lightly and gave me a thumbs up below the table. I took a deep breath and nodded. We had this.

The main door to the conference room opened and I turned as Callie did to see our competition. We both gasped as we watched Ashley prance into the room followed by a very nerdy middle-aged man who looked around nervously as he walked in. She was wearing a low-cut blouse that barely covered her pushed-up assets and a skirt so tight I wondered how she'd be able to sit. Mr. Davenport stood and approached Ashley, who was now staring at us obviously as dumbfounded as we were.

"Miss Blankenship, Mr. Chase, welcome. As you can see, I have representatives from ABC Designs to present their proposal as well. We are all here now and can begin the meeting." Tristan seated Ashley, who had somewhat regained her composure but was eyeing Callie's belly and wedding ring and she smirked. I clenched my fist and felt Callie touch my arm. She looked at me and mouthed 'It's okay. I took a deep breath and let it go slowly. We had a job to do and blowing Ashley out of the water was now priority number one. Mr. Davenport gestured for Ashley to do her presentation first. She stood making a point to exaggerate her cleavage as she did. I noticed the old man who'd been about to nap suddenly took notice but the woman wrinkled her nose with distaste, which made me smile. Ashley snapped her fingers and the nerdy guy, who I assume was the Chase in Grayson/Chase, jumped to start the PowerPoint. I watched him gazing at her and could only assume that he was reaping the benefits of her bed so she could get a leg up (pun intended) in the firm. Ashley deliberately took her time sashaying to the head of the table eventually to stand next to Mr. Davenport. She put her hand on his shoulder giving it a squeeze and I couldn't help but wrinkle my nose too. Really? She was definitely pouring on the sex appeal in buckets. I felt Callie tense up next to me and now it was my turn to calm her down. We needed our heads to be clear for this or Ashley would win and that just wasn't happening.

"Gentlemen." She paused for effect. "And ladies." She smirked again. I'm here representing Grayson and Chase to propose our design for your new bank building." She began to outline the building layout, and I knew right away it wasn't going to work. Jay had been very specific in taking the client's wants and incorporating them into his design. Her design looked like she was making a resort not a professional bank building. I poked Callie under the table and threw her a smile. She flashed an evil grin, and I was glad to see she was getting her head in the game. We listened as Ashley droned on about mood lighting and a soothing waterfall in the lobby. Callie smirked at the waterfall. I knew that was one thing she hated putting in unless the client insisted. Mr. Davenport had specifically said he didn't want one for maintenance purposes. I began to wonder if Ashley even met with him. She hadn't gotten one thing right about the design.

"And this concludes our proposal. We hope you will consider it." She threw out a dazzling smile as she squeezed Mr. Davenport's shoulder one last time. There was a smattering of applause from the older man and Mr. Chase. She strutted back to her chair and stood waiting for Tristan to hop over to pull it out, but he stayed at his position near the door engrossed in something on his phone. She finally snapped her fingers and her boy toy Chase hopped into action sliding it out for her. As she tried to sit as seductively as possible, she misjudged the edge of the chair and plopped right down on the floor. I was biting my tongue so hard I almost bit it in half trying not to laugh. I could see Callie's shoulders shaking and knew she was just seconds from losing it. Ashley, still trying to get the hot guy to notice her, held out her hand toward Tristan, but now he seemed to be busy typing something on his iPad so she huffed and threw her hand out to Mr. Chase. He was all over that in a second making sure to place his hands on the parts that really didn't help her get up. I was holding my breath at this point because I knew I was on the verge of snorting. She finally managed to get situated in the chair and the whole time this was going on Mr. Davenport's expression got darker and darker. I started praying that it wouldn't affect his mood for our presentation.

He stood and motioned toward Ashley. "Thank you, Miss Blankenship. I must say, these plans are a huge surprise to me. I don't even recall asking for some of these things," he said somewhat sarcastically. He now gestured toward Callie. "Mrs. Brisson, you have the floor." He sat back in his chair and smiled.

Callie stood and began. "Mr. Davenport, Mr. Jackson, Mrs. Stanton. I am representing ABC Designs and would like to show you our proposal for your new bank building." I looked at her in amazement. My girl had done her research. She began the PowerPoint presentation and was flawless. If I could have stood and cheered as she spoke, I would have. "As you can see by the plans drawn by my partner, Jay Anderson, we incorporated the professional image you desired by using a minimalistic approach." She pointed out the features that Mr. Davenport had made clear he wanted and I could see his smile getting bigger. I also saw Ashley beginning to get agitated. Awesome. Apparently, karma was a bitch just like her and I wanted it to bite her in the ass. After showing the final computer rendering, Callie began wrapping up her presentation. "In conclusion, ladies and gentlemen, our budget was five million and with the eco-friendly modifications we've added, we can bring it in at around three." Callie smiled and moved to sit down as Mr. Davenport began applauding. Everyone joined in including Mr. Chase which made Ashley livid. Tristan and I were the loudest and I even think I whistled.

"Well, I think we have a clear winner here." Mr. Davenport said rising from his chair. "George...Susan? Are we in agreement?" The partners were nodding as Mr. Davenport walked over to us and gave Callie and me hearty handshakes. "Congratulations ABC Designs. You've got our building." He gestured to the others in the room and everyone took leave except for Mr. Chase and Ashley.

Callie and I were packing up our things when I heard Ashley bark, "Ron, be a darling and wait at the car." He grabbed their things and sped out of the room leaving the three of us alone. I was hyper-aware of the tension in the room. She sauntered over and leaned her hip against the table. "So, Callie. How've you been? It seems you've put on some *weight* since I saw you last." When she'd emphasized the word weight, I saw Callie flinch. "Guess it's just a matter of time before Justin starts looking for something..." she paused as she slid her hands up and down her hips, "more attractive."

Oh no, she didn't! Callie started to speak but in an instant I found myself inches from Ashley's nose. "You need to back off," I said between clenched teeth. "Justin loves Callie and as you can see they have a baby on the way."

Ashley looked at me down her nose and snorted. "Is that what it is? I just thought she was fat," she said laughing.

The next thing I heard was the crack of my palm meeting her left cheek. Ashley grabbed her face with her hand and pouted her lips. "What are you, her damn bodyguard?" She hissed.

"No, bitch. I'm her best friend," I said grabbing Callie by the arm and propelling her out the door. We started down the hall and ran into Tristan who was headed back to the conference room.

"I hope everything went okay in there," he said gesturing toward the door. "I sensed a little tension between you."

"You have no idea, Tristan," Callie said with a big grin. "Everything is awesome and I'm taking my best friend shopping for lingerie. I owe her big time!"

Chapter 9

Callie insisted on taking me straight to Victoria's Secret to get some sexy lingerie for my potential weekend getaway, which hadn't even been planned yet. Once in the store, I texted Jay to tell him we got the job and he responded immediately that he was so proud of us and that we needed to plan a celebration. Callie snatched my phone and texted...

We could go away for a weekend alone hot stuff

She hit send before I could stop her and she smacked me on the butt and told me to shut it. Literally twenty seconds later, he texted back...

That looked like something Callie would write. But thank her because I think it's an awesome plan, can't wait!

My mouth fell open. Callie started laughing. "Easy peasy, you big chicken." She found a salesperson and told her I needed to be set up for a romantic weekend. Every available person in the store flocked around us as Callie, waving her credit card, pulled a "Pretty Woman" and told the girls to fix me up. They brought out bustier and panty sets, frilly sheer babydoll nighties, and teddys with garters. Callie insisted I trash the oversized t-shirt I slept in and raise the hot factor.   I'd been on my own so long I'd never needed sexy things, but Callie reminded me of the handsome green-eyed hunk who'd already warmed my bed once and was ready for a repeat.   I flushed thinking of that night, remembering how passionate and sexy I'd felt and how I really wanted it to happen again and again.

Callie plopped herself on a chair near the dressing rooms putting her feet up on a box of bras. I would open the door and get a thumbs up or down. Callie seemed to like everything, but I wasn't so sure. I could see my bulges in some of the really snug things and was self-conscious. I finally decided on two different sets giving me a variety of choices. The first outfit was a red sheer babydoll nightie with a matching thong. This was the most modest of the four and Callie named that my granny nightie. I didn't want to imagine any granny in that kind of nightwear. The second was a white bustier trimmed in black lace. It was a garter style which I paired with matching panties and black sheer stockings. Callie REALLY liked this one and she even whistled when I walked out. "Girl, you need some black stilettos to go with that outfit!" She said waggling her eyebrows. A salesperson hovering nearby dashed off to return with a pair in my size. I slipped them on and realized they had to have at least a five inch heel.

"How the hell am I supposed to walk in these?" I said wobbling across the floor to look in the mirror.

"You don't have to walk! Jay will carry you to bed, probably over his shoulder like a caveman!" She said laughing. I just shook my head.

"How is this even considered clothing?" I lamented. Callie was on the phone with Justin and did the zip-it thing with her mouth. I pouted and she shook her finger at me. The fact it was the middle finger actually hurt my feelings, well a little anyway. At the last minute, Callie grabbed a satin black robe off the rack. She was ecstatic over the possibility of my wearing it as a robe over one of my other choices or by itself. She seemed to be living vicariously through me and that thought cracked me up. Exhausted, she slowly got up off her chair and paid for the entire shopping spree despite my protests.

"Jane, today we landed a huge client and you played a very important part in that. Let me treat you. I love you and you deserve even more than this," she said scooping up some of the lighter bags. "You and Jay deserve some happiness too."

"Woman, I love you," I said grabbing the rest of the bags. I dropped her off at her place and called Jay. He squeaked a hello.

"Hey, I was calling to see if you wanted anything to eat or drink. I could stop by on the way to pick up Jolene." Honestly, I just wanted to see him. I kept my fingers crossed.

"Actually, I could use some Vick's rubbed on my chest. You up for that?" He asked laughing while pretending to cough.

"I am totally up for that. I'll use any excuse to rub that chest." I giggled. "Seriously, if you need me, I'll stop by."

"No, baby. I still don't want to risk Jolene catching this. However, I will take you up on the chest rub when I feel better. What's this about a weekend away? Were you serious? I would love to go away for a weekend alone with you."

"Sure, Callie volunteered to babysit so I'd love to, whenever you feel better," I said pulling up in front of the daycare.

"I'm feeling better already. I'll make some arrangements, anywhere special you want to go?"

"Well, not too far in case of an emergency. Callie and Justin are going to babysit.   Do you know any nice places nearby?"

"As a matter of fact, I have a friend who owns a cabin not twenty minutes from town. It's recently been renovated. I'll give him a call and see when it's available. How's that sound?"

"Sounds heavenly. I think I need to drop off a case of antibiotics so you can get better quick!" I said laughing.

"Believe me, a weekend with you as my incentive, I'll be better in no time."

"Well, you take care. Callie and I will take care of things at the office. If we need you for anything, we'll call."

"You too, baby. I'm missing you something fierce," he said softly.

I closed my eyes imagining him whispering in my ear. "I miss you too," I whispered. "See you soon."

I walked into the daycare and saw the owner, Mrs. Bloom walking toward me. "Ms. Carter, we need to talk." She gestured me into one of the play rooms and shut the door. "We had an incident today. A man claiming to be Jolene's father came here demanding to pick her up." The blood rushed from my face. "We were so thankful you'd given us a heads up about not releasing her to anyone. We told him that we didn't have a child here by that name and even if we did, he'd have no authority to pick her up."

I took a deep breath. "It had to be her father, Tyler. I can't believe he is being so persistent. He's really scaring me now."

"Well, I don't know the history between you two but from the sound of things, he's not planning just to go away," she said placing her hand on my arm. "Jolene was never in danger. I promise."

I heard voices approaching and then a knock at the door. It was Jolene with her teacher, Traci. "Mama!" Jolene squealed with delight. "Miss Traci let us watch my favorite movie today."

Traci nodded. "We watched "Tangled" and I swear she knows every word. I was amazed. She certainly is a smart little girl." So relieved to see she was safely with me, I pulled her close and gave her a big hug. She squirmed in my arms, giggling. I was going to have to take care of this once and for all. I would have to confront Tyler and see exactly what his intentions were. I called Callie and asked if I could drop Jolene off for a little bit and as always, she said yes. I didn't say anything to her about what had happened because I knew she'd tell me not to talk to him but I had to do something. After seeing Jolene safely inside the condo, I sat in my car and with shaking hands I called the number Tyler had given me.

Chapter 10

He answered almost immediately.

"Tyler, it's Jane," I said angrily.

"I knew you'd call. I had to do something to get your attention and I guess it worked." He sounded triumphant.

"What do you want?" I asked through gritted teeth. "What are you trying to do?"

"I want to talk. I need to have some time with you to show you how much I've changed. I won't stop showing up where Jolene is until you take the time to talk to me."

I paused. I couldn't see any other way out of this. "I can meet you somewhere. Tyler, we need to get this over with. Where are you?"

"I'm still at the same motel. Will you meet me here?" He pleaded.

I didn't feel good about that at all. "I'd rather meet you in a public place. We can meet at the park where you saw us the other day. Meet me by the swings in half an hour."

"Okay, thank you, Jane. You won't regret this. I'd never hurt you or Jolene, I just want a chance. I'll see you then." I hung up the phone and sat staring at it. What was I thinking? I needed to tell someone where I was going, but I knew that if I did they'd stop me. As I started my car, that thought wouldn't leave my head.

I pulled up at the park and didn't see anyone around. It had been a dreary day so it had deterred even the die-hard joggers from doing their laps. I got out and walked over to the swings and sat down on one. Swinging back and forth, my mind kept screaming at me that I was all alone. I didn't think Tyler would hurt me but I hadn't thought he'd leave me pregnant either. I seemed to be a great judge of character. I heard a car. I turned to see him pull up and at the last minute, I texted Callie.

I'm at the park with Tyler. I needed to let you know.

I looked up to see him approaching. He was glancing around nervously as if I had a SWAT team positioned in the trees waiting for him. Standing as he got closer, I said, "I'm alone Tyler, if that's what you're worried about."

He seemed relieved. "Well, I didn't know if you'd bring Callie or that new boyfriend of yours for protection."

"Why would I need protection?" I asked sitting back down on the swing. "You aren't dangerous, are you?" I ignored the boyfriend comment for now.

"No, I'm not dangerous. I've just been desperate to talk to you and you've been avoiding me. I had to make something happen. I'm running out of money and I need to know if we're going to be together." He sounded desperate.

"Tyler, did you come here intending to live with me? Did you think all that happened in the past would be forgotten? I'm not the same person you left five years ago. I'm stronger now and very protective of my child."

"I can tell you aren't the same. You used to look at me like I was your whole world, but now you look at me as if I was a piece of dirt. I can see it, Jane. The thing is, I've changed and I'm willing to work things out and be a husband to you and a father to Jolene."

I stared at him with my mouth open. "Husband? Father? Seriously? Tyler, you are living in a fantasy world. You seem to have conveniently forgotten all that's happened. Where were you all these years? You knew where I was but you never once called to check on me. I went through my pregnancy with Callie's support. She went to my ultrasound appointments with me, and she drove me to the hospital when I was in labor. You weren't there for me. When Jolene was born, I should've been in the hospital sharing that moment with you. Instead, I was alone. When Jolene cried in the middle of the night, I was the only one there to feed and change her. Not a day went by that I didn't worry what would happen to her if, God forbid, something happened to me. My family abandoned me because I chose you, so I had nobody. I've been alone through Jolene's first steps, first word, first everything. I can't see myself loving you again Tyler. You broke that love the day you walked away leaving me that note." I felt my voice break so I took a deep breath.

"I know, I thought I was doing the right thing by leaving. I was so messed up with drugs and alcohol at the time. I thought it'd be better to run away from you and my responsibilities. I never once thought about how this would affect you. My sole focus was where my next fix would come from. I was sitting at a bus stop, drinking a beer when I saw a man come up to wait for the bus. He had a little boy with him and when they saw me, the man pulled the child away from the shelter. I was so embarrassed the man wouldn't trust me next to him, I quit drinking right then. It took me a few months more to kick the drugs with the help of a support group. During one of the meetings, they asked us was there one thing we regretted missing out on the most while using. My mind flashed to you and our kid. I didn't know whether it was a he or a she and it bothered me. That boy at the bus stop could have been mine with a stepdad watching him grow up and I would never know. That's when I decided to come looking for you. Jane, I wish I could turn back the clock and be there for all those things, but I can't. I know this, though, I still love you. That never went away." I felt tears brimming in my eyes, so I looked across the park to avoid looking at him. He knelt in front of me and wrapped his hands around mine. "Jane, do you still love me? Do you have any feelings left for me?"

I looked at him and felt nothing but confusion. I'd loved him for so long I wasn't sure if it had really gone away. "Tyler, I..."

"Let her go."

I looked over to see Jay standing just a few feet away. His voice was strong. Tyler jumped to his feet, backing away from me. "What business is it of yours, man? This is a private conversation."

Jay moved to tower over Tyler, looking at him with obvious disgust. "It's very much my business," Jay said putting himself between me and Tyler. "I think you need to pack your shit and leave town, if you know what's good for you." Glancing back at me he said, "You okay?"

I nodded. Jay stepped forward. "Consider this a warning. You come around Jane or Jolene again and you'll be dealing with me. I'm not going to let you come back into their lives and mess with their heads."

Tyler looked around Jay toward me. "Jane, is that what you want? It didn't seem like that a few minutes ago. I was getting the vibe that you still loved me, that you were willing to give me another chance."

I saw Jay's body tense. I knew it was time to be strong. "Tyler, whatever vibe you got was wrong. I've moved on. I'm happier without you in my life. Please, just leave us alone." I felt a tear slide down my cheek. Jay reached his hand back and I took it. Squeezing it gently, he pulled me to stand beside him.

Tyler stood staring at the two of us for a moment then shook his head. "Jane, I tried to reason with you. I warned you that this could get ugly. I guess we'll have to do this the hard way. I'm not going away that easily. I'll get a lawyer and I'll get Jolene. You'll regret this." He turned on his heel and walked away, glancing back periodically all the way back to his car.

Jay pulled me close. "You okay?" He kissed the top of my head.

My body began to tremble uncontrollably. I wrapped my arms around him and held on tight. "Callie told you, didn't she?" I whispered.

He rested his chin on the top of my head. I could feel him nod. "She was afraid he'd hurt you. I'm glad she called me. I wish you'd have trusted me enough to let me know what was happening."

I pulled away to look up into his eyes. "Jay, I'd intended to tell you, but with you being sick I decided to wait until I could tell you in person. Coming here alone was a stupid move on my part and that's why I texted Callie at the last minute."

He took a deep breath. "I don't know what I would've done if he'd hurt you. You and Jolene have become so important to me. I can't help feeling protective. I'm sorry if that scares or upsets you."

I hugged him tighter and laid my head against his chest. "You make me feel so safe. I'm not scared or upset at all." I looked back up at him. "I've had to look out for Jolene and myself for so long, it's strange to have someone else want to do it."

"Jane, about what he said. I need to ask you something important. Is Tyler on Jolene's birth certificate as her father?"

"No, he'd have had to sign the birth certificate if I'd listed him, so I didn't put a father. It's marked unknown," I said. Suddenly, I was thinking back to the day in the hospital when I had to sign the paperwork and the sadness I felt knowing that I had to leave that space blank.

"Well, I know for a fact if he tries to go to court to get Jolene, he'll have to submit to DNA testing to determine if he's her biological father. Do you think he has enough money to hire a lawyer and do all the testing?" Jay questioned.

"I don't know. I doubt it. He just told me a few minutes ago that he was running low on money and he needed to find out soon what I wanted," I said honestly.

"He may be just looking for a payoff. He probably assumes you're making a good living now and is trying to work his way back in so you can support him. He's using Jolene as leverage." He cupped my face with his strong hand and gently stroked my bottom lip with his thumb. "I won't let him hurt you or Jolene. I swear it." I knew looking into his eyes that he meant every word. I wanted to kiss him so badly at that moment. Instead, I gently kissed his cheek. He smiled and whispered, "I'm gonna want that kiss when I get better." He wrapped his arm around my shoulders and walked me back to my car. Jay followed me back to Callie's so I could collect Jolene. He walked me upstairs making sure I was safely to the door. Kissing my forehead and giving me another hug, he said goodnight. Watching him walk down the stairs, my heart melted. What an awesome guy.

Chapter 11

I heard Mrs. Callahan's door open. "You okay, sweetie? I was taking Garth out earlier and overheard some of what was going on." She touched my arm. "I'm glad to see you're safe."

"I'm fine and thanks for your concern, Mrs. Callahan." I gave her a hug.

"I've gotten attached to you girls. I want only happiness for you both." She patted my cheek and went back into her apartment. Callie must have been watching through the peephole because as soon as she left, she opened the door.

"Are you out of your mind?" Callie said grabbing me into a tight hug. I'd expected her to be spitting mad, but she seemed more upset than anything.

"I know, I was stupid. I should have never gone alone." I looked at my best friend who was nodding her head in agreement with everything I said. "And thank you for telling Jay."

"Girl, when I got that text...you can ask Justin...I was flipping a wig! I didn't know what else to do! I knew he'd want to know." She snatched me by the arm and dragged me to their bedroom. Shutting the door behind her, she turned and with a serious look said, "So, what in the hell did he want?"

I closed my eyes and took a deep breath. "He was trying to get me back. He claims he's off the drugs and alcohol and he wants another chance," I said waiting for Callie's reaction.

She stood looking at me for a moment then said, "Jane, I don't think for one minute that he's changed. There's something fishy about him showing up now after all this time. I don't like how he's approached you either. It's almost like he's manipulating you through Jolene."

"Jay said the same thing. He thinks Tyler is using her as leverage," I said plopping onto the bed. "I'm just so mentally exhausted by this whole situation."

Sitting on the bed beside me, she elbowed me gently. "Jane, you know we're best friends and I would never say anything that might jeopardize that but are you still in love with Tyler? You seem so torn and if you've really put him in the past, you wouldn't be feeling so conflicted."

I shook my head. "To be honest, I really was confused when I saw Tyler one on one and heard him apologize for everything. He seemed sincere but when Jay showed up putting himself literally between us, he showed his true colors." I paused to take a deep breath. "He threatened to get a lawyer and take Jolene."

Callie's mouth dropped open. "He's lost it. There is no way in hell he can get Jolene, can he?" Now she looked worried.

"Jay said that Tyler would have to petition the court for a DNA test to prove he's the father since I didn't list him on the birth certificate. Honestly, I don't think he has the money for the lawyer or the test." I lay back on the bed and rubbed my eyes with the palms of my hands. "I think he's just trying to force my hand. He has to know I don't have the money to fight him if he can somehow get this into court."

"Well, if it comes down to a court battle, you'll have all the financial support Justin and I can give. We won't let Jolene go anywhere," she said rubbing my arm. "You're a part of our family and we'll stand by you."

I kept rubbing my eyes now to stop the flow of tears that sprang forth when she said that. I took a shuddering breath. Callie didn't say anything. She grabbed my arm, pulled me up and hugged me tight. We sat that way for a while, me sobbing silently on her shoulder while she rubbed my back. We heard a knock at the door, and I sat back and wiped my eyes with the back of my hand.

Justin stuck his head in. "You okay, Jane?" When I nodded he walked over to me and knelt in front of me. "I know Callie's probably already told you but whatever you need, we're here for you."

"I love you guys." We all stood and embraced in a group hug. "I don't know what I'd do without you."

Callie spoke, "Well, it's a good thing you never have to find out. We're not going anywhere."

"Well, I'd better get my little girl home. It's been a long day for her too." I walked to the living room where Jolene was still fast asleep. Looking at her, for the first time, I clearly saw myself. All these years I'd been looking for signs of Tyler but never gave myself any credit for this beautiful child. From her long eyelashes that fanned her slightly freckled cheeks to her ears with the tiny lobes that were identical to mine. She was my mini-me. Callie came up and put her arm around me and we stood watching the soft rise and fall of her chest as she slept.

Justin walked up and touched my arm. Whispering, he said, "Jane, I'm going to follow you to your apartment. I had to promise Jay I'd get you home so no arguments, okay?

Justin gently scooped Jolene into his arms. She stirred just a little but tucked her face against his shoulder and proceeded to snore. Lightly touching her hair, Callie pressed a light kiss to her forehead. I grabbed her bag and followed Justin down to my car. He looked around cautiously as he bundled her into her car seat. She murmured, rolled her head to the side and started snoring again. I got in my car and locked the doors. He got in his car and followed me to my apartment. I'd gathered Jolene into my arms by the time he parked. He took my keys and my bag and walked me to the door. He was just unlocking it when Maegan opened her door. "Hey, Jane. I wanted to let you know, some guy came by here just a little while ago looking for you. He was banging on your door, yelling your name. He sounded drunk so I didn't open my door. He finally left but I thought I should tell you."

Justin pulled out his phone and started texting. He looked at me seriously. "Do you need to stay with us? You can pack a bag and stay as long as you need to."

"No, Justin. I'm not going to run and hide. I'll be okay. Thanks for letting me know, Maegan." She nodded and went back into her apartment.

Justin motioned for me to stay at the door while he went inside to make sure there was no danger. When he gestured it was okay, I took Jolene to her room, slipped off her shoes and left her in her clothes, so I wouldn't wake her. I got her tucked in with her doll and joined Justin back in the living room.

"I've texted Jay. He's on his way over," he said holding his finger up to stop any argument. I didn't argue. I was just too exhausted. Within a few minutes, a knock came at the door making me jump. Justin walked to the door, looked out the peephole and opened it.

Jay came rushing in. "Is everything okay?" He asked looking at me closely to make sure I was in one piece. He gave me a hug.

"I'm fine. I don't think he'll be back tonight. My guess is he's passed out somewhere sleeping it off. Do you guys want anything to drink? Hot chocolate? Coffee?" I headed towards the kitchen. I saw them both shake their heads no as they started talking quietly. I made myself a big mug of hot chocolate and was adding some milk to cool it down when Jay came into the kitchen. He leaned against the counter watching me.

"Justin left. We both agree it's best if I stay here in case Tyler shows up again." He shook his head. "He just doesn't want to let go, does he?"

I took a sip of my hot chocolate before speaking. "Jay, I don't think it's that he wants me or Jolene for that matter. I think he just wants the life he could have had before he screwed it all up with his wild ways. He told me he wished he could go back and change everything but he knows that can't happen.

His way of dealing with it is to try to make our lives miserable."

He looked at me and in his eyes, I saw such compassion and caring that my heart skipped a beat. He took the cup from my hand and set it on the counter. He pulled me close, wrapping his arms around me. I lay my head on his chest breathing in his clean fresh scent. His chest rumbled against my ear as he spoke, "I've missed being with you."

I snuggled closer pressing my body up against his. "I've missed this," I whispered. Reluctantly, I pulled away. I was so emotionally and physically tired I couldn't keep my eyes open. Jay went to the linen closet, grabbed the blanket and pillow that we usually shared and made his bed on the couch. I hugged him tightly once more, wandered into my room and threw myself on the bed. Within moments, just knowing he was nearby, I was fast asleep.

Chapter 12

The next morning, I heard a high pitched squeal which signaled Jolene's discovery of Jay on the couch. I jumped up and ran to the living room. Jolene was clapping and bouncing up and down in front him. He was obviously half-awake but managed to smile. "Jolene," he said, "don't come too close because I've been sick and I don't want you to get it."

Her eyes grew wide. "Sick? I don't wanna get sick," she said moving back a step. She hadn't noticed me yet. I came up behind her and started tickling her. She giggled trying to get away. "Mama, stop it!" She said still giggling. Jay was laughing watching her squirm.

"Okay, I'll stop." I let her go and just as she was going to be out of reach, I grabbed her and tickled her again. She was squealing by now and she had me laughing out loud as well. Finally I said, "We need to get some breakfast and get you ready to go to daycare."

Jolene threw out her bottom lip. "But Mama, I wanna stay with you and Jay."

Jay looked at her quivering lip. "Boy, she sure knows how to use that thing to her advantage, doesn't she?" He pretended to be studying it. Jolene tried not to laugh but his expression was so serious that she finally couldn't hold the lip out any longer. She threw back her head and laughed. "Jane, I think Jolene's earned a trip to work with us today." He raised his brows and I knew exactly what he was thinking. Jolene would be safer with us.

"Are you going in to work? Aren't you still feeling bad?" I said starting the coffee and getting Jolene some cereal. Jay grabbed a pair of mugs out of my cupboard and set them beside the coffee maker.

"I'm actually feeling a lot better this morning," he said waggling his eyebrows up and down while making puckers with his lips. Jolene was behind him and couldn't see, but I could, and I rolled my eyes and giggled. Jay poured our coffee as I watched in amazement as my child ate every bite of her breakfast.

She put her bowl in the sink then headed to her bedroom. I turned on the small tv in the kitchen, and we sat, legs entwined, watching the morning news. The news reporter was talking about a zoning case and how the locals were upset about a cheap tobacco place being put in the middle of a pretty classy neighborhood.   The next story started and I really wasn't paying attention because Jay had taken my foot, put it in his lap and was massaging it.   Suddenly, something the reporter said got my attention big time. "Local architects to marry, details after these messages." We watched about five useless commercials and the reporter was back. "Mr. Ron Chase from the architecture firm, Grayson and Chase has announced his intention to marry fellow architect and co-worker, Ashley Blankenship. This will be Mr. Chase's second marriage following his recent divorce from his wife of twenty years, and Miss Blankenship's first. The wedding will take place at Mr. Chase's estate, Brookshire Crossing in two months. This will be the second wedding of local architects in just a few short months, the most recent being that of Mr. and Mrs. Justin Brisson from Xenia and ABC Designs.

"Oh my God," I said staring at the tv. Jay looked at me with a confused look on his face. "I never got a chance to tell you everything that happened at the Davenport meeting." I gave Jay a blow by blow account of the meeting and then told him about our encounter after we'd won the account. His eyes grew wide as he heard about my reaction to Ashley's insults to Callie and my subsequent hand to cheek response. I waited for him to become angry, but instead he shook his head and started chuckling. I assured him that Mr. Davenport was nowhere near the conference room when this went down. The only ones who knew were the three of us and Tristan, who'd actually seemed pretty pleased about it. I had to tell Callie about Ashley's big news. I texted Callie...

You watch the news? Ashley's getting married.

What? No way!

Yup. She bagged a partner! Chase is biting the dust, bless his heart.

Sucker!

"Mama, I'm ready for work." I heard from Jolene's bedroom.

See you in a little bit. Jolene's coming with us today.

I threw my phone in my purse. Walking into her room, I stopped dead in my tracks. She was completely naked except for a pair of my pantyhose which she had pulled up under her arms.

I didn't want to make her feel embarrassed, but it was hard to keep a straight face. "Sweetie, is that what you think I wear to work?" I said stifling a giggle.

With a totally serious expression she said, "Don't be silly, Mama. I still got to put on my shoes." She'd gone in my closet and found the five inch stilettos that went with my sexy lingerie and was attempting to put them on.

"Baby, I can assure you, I wouldn't wear those shoes to work. My feet would hurt so badly by the end of the day." I was struggling to keep my composure especially seeing how serious she was. "Tell you what, we'll find an outfit in your closet that looks like my work clothes and I'll let you wear one of my grown-up necklaces with it. Deal?"

She thought about it for a moment then nodded. "Deal." I helped her get out of the pantyhose and dug around in her closet. I found a dress that I'd gotten at a clearance sale a few months back. It had been too big at the time but now was just right. She had one pair of dressy shoes that were on the verge of being too small but were workable for today. I took her to my bedroom and pulled out my jewelry box. I had several necklaces that were costume, so I set them out on the dresser and let her choose. Being my daughter and having excellent taste, she went for the diamonds. Thank God they weren't real, but she didn't know that and she was squealing with delight when I clasped them around her neck. "I wanna show Jay," she said dashing out to show off her work clothes. I heard him chatting with her about her outfit, so I threw myself in the shower to get ready.

Upon arriving at work, I explained to Callie how I felt safer having Jolene in sight. She agreed especially having heard the whole story from Justin the night before. Having a four year old at work was a mixed blessing. I loved having her close by but honestly, I didn't know how she could talk non-stop all day. Everything I did she had to ask why. When I explained, she'd say why again. I could feel my hair turning gray as the day went on. Callie and Jay stayed busy in their offices which left us to entertain ourselves. I finally gave her the task of untangling my paperclips. That kept her busy for a while especially since they were in one big clump. She sat in a chair across from my desk with her tongue sticking out the side of her mouth as she struggled to pull them apart. I saw Callie poke her head out of her office and she had to cover her mouth to stifle a giggle. I just smiled and shrugged. She was happy, that was the important thing.

I was just fishing out a ball of rubber bands for her to untangle when the phone rang. "ABC Designs, Jane Carter speaking." The caller hesitated. "Hello?" I tried again.

"Is Jay in?" It was a female voice. I looked around behind me and saw Jay was tied up on the phone.

"I'm sorry, he's on the phone, may I take a message?" I asked watching Jolene pull the first rubber band free with a grin.

"Well, I don't have time to call back. Um…tell him that Meredith called. The test ruled him out. He'll know what that means…and tell him thank you." She hung up.

I sat there for a moment processing the message I'd written down on the scratch pad. *Meredith called. The test ruled you out. Thank you*. Ruled him out of what? And who was Meredith? My thoughts were interrupted by Jolene poking me to point out she had two rubber bands free now. I nodded, patted her head and glanced back at Jay who was just finishing up his phone call. "Jolene, can you be a good girl and sit here while I talk to Jay?" I asked grabbing the note. She nodded, never taking her eyes off the rubber band knot. I knocked on the door and Jay beckoned me in. I didn't say anything, I just put the note down. He smiled looking up at me then down at the note. I watched the blood drain from his face. He looked out at Jolene sitting at the desk then back at me. "I'll be at my desk if you need me," I said turning to go.

"Don't leave. Please sit. I needed to tell you about this and now is as good a time as ever."   He took a deep breath, held it then blew it out. "Jane, this is something that's been on my mind for months. You probably don't remember but I got a phone call a while back that upset me.   You asked me about it at the time but I said it was nothing."

I remembered that phone call. I'd told Callie about it and how weird it was. He'd acted so distant after that until the wedding reception. "Yes, I remember," I said feeling my heart hammering in my chest.

"Well, a few years ago, before I moved to Asheville, I lived in Raleigh. I met a woman named Meredith and we ended up dating for about six months. Toward the end of our relationship, there were subtle hints that our relationship was fizzling out but nothing definite until she called me on the phone one day and told me it was over. I never heard from her again...until that phone call." He paused to look at the piece of paper the message was written on. He took another deep breath. "She called to tell me that I might be the father of her child."

I felt my mouth drop open. In my heart, I probably expected this but hearing it confirmed was something entirely different. "Jay, why didn't you tell me then?"

His eyes were so sad. "I didn't want to risk losing you. My feelings for you were growing every day and I was getting attached to Jolene. I didn't want to jeopardize that."

"Jay, things happen. Why would my feelings change? If anything, I'd be more supportive of you being a part of the child's life. I've been down the deadbeat dad road with Tyler."

His expression grew serious. "I thought I could handle it without causing anyone any harm. I decided to back away from you and Jolene but my feelings for you were too strong. That's why I apologized at the reception."

I blushed thinking of that night. "So, you've resolved this with Meredith?"

"Yes, that's how I know so much about birth certificates and paternity claims. She needed money and decided to once and for all figure out who the real father was for support money. Apparently there was another man in the running. She'd been cheating on me. I didn't know it at the time, but she was. We'd always used protection, but she convinced me that there was a chance it didn't work so I decided the best thing was to find out for sure." He paused. "I took the test about a week ago. Apparently the results came back excluding me." His shoulders slumped with relief.

I sat there for a moment absorbing everything. "Jay, let me tell you something. I really care about you and if you'd found out you were the child's father, I would've been here to support you. That wouldn't make me leave."

He reached out his hand and I took it. He pulled me out of the chair to embrace me tightly. "Thank you," he whispered. "You don't know what that means to me."

"Mama!" Pulling away from Jay, I turned to see Jolene holding up another rubber band.

I smiled and waved at her. "Good job, baby!" I turned back to Jay. "I'm as guilty of hiding things as you are. I should've told you about Tyler from the beginning but I felt you'd probably shy away from my "baby daddy" drama. As it turns out, you've gone above and beyond to protect Jolene and me. I can't thank you enough."

"Having you and Jolene safe is all the thanks I need." He looked out at my little girl and his face softened. "I still can't believe that man could walk away from such a precious gift. He's an even bigger fool for leaving you." His jaw tightened. "I wanted to pound him into the dirt when I saw him standing there smugly claiming you still wanted to be with him."

I took a deep breath. "I was letting him get to me when you got there. I saw glimpses of the old Tyler and it started to pull at my heart but when I saw you, I knew…" I stopped.

"Knew what, Jane? Tell me, please." He stepped closer.

"I knew that…" I couldn't say it. I was so scared of being rejected again. It had me emotionally paralyzed.

"I hope you're going to say you love me because if you do, I'll be the happiest man on earth." He smiled tucking a piece of hair behind my ear.

I felt tears welling up and I blinked to try to stop them. I blew out a breath. "I really do. I'm so afraid of what that means, but I really do." I smiled and felt a tear roll down my cheek. He gently wiped it away.

"Jane, I'll be right beside you through whatever Tyler throws at you. I can't imagine my life without you…or Sweet Pea." He motioned to the door where Jolene was standing with a handful of rubber bands. She came running in towards Jay when she heard him use his nickname for her, and he scooped her up. She wrapped her arm around his neck and leaned her forehead against his. My heart melted watching the love in his eyes.

"Mama?" She said looking at me. "Did I do good today?" I reached up, squeezed her cheeks gently making her lips pucker. I gave her a big kiss making her giggle.

"Yes, baby. I'm so proud of you for being a big girl. I love you." Hearing a light knock at the door, we turned to see Callie standing there.

"So, is Jolene going to stay with Aunt Callie and Uncle Justin soon? I think I want to spoil my little pea pod." She grinned.

Jolene started squealing. "Mama! I wanna go! Pleeeease?"

Jay's eyes met mine and his eyebrows rose in question. I pretended to think about it but my racing heart was thundering in my ears. "Well, I guess it would be okay...but you have to promise you'll be a good girl and listen to Aunt Callie and do what she says. Deal?"

Jolene squealed again. "Deal, Mama!" She squirmed out of Jay's arms and ran to Callie where she laid her head on Callie's expanding belly. "Ryder! I get to come stay with you!"

We all looked at Jolene with confusion. "Ryder?" I asked. "Jolene, where did you get that name?"

"Don't you know, Mama? It's in my favorite movie. I like his name. It's Rapunzel's boyfriend," she said it so matter of fact that we all started laughing.

Callie gazed down at Jolene. "You know, I think we're going to run that name by Uncle Justin. I kinda like it!" She started chuckling. "The baby just kicked hard. I think he likes it too. Come with me Jolene, we're going to call Uncle Justin right now and you can tell him the name you like." Jolene bounced up and down clapping her hands. As they left the office, Callie pulled the door shut with a wink.

Jay sat on the edge of the desk and pulled me close. "I've got some important work to do. I have to plan a spectacular weekend for the woman I love."

Giving him a puzzled look I said, "Anyone I know?" He responded by capturing my mouth and pulling me tightly against him, his hands spanning my lower back. This kiss was different. It was possessive but gentle and it captured my heart. Breathless, I finally broke the kiss whispering in his ear, "I think she's a very lucky woman."

Shaking his head, he said giving me tender kisses on my neck, "I'm a very lucky man. I'm going to get on the phone and see when I can steal you away." He reluctantly let me go.

"I'm going to go check on Jolene. Let me know what you find out." I gave him a wink and headed to Callie's office.

Standing at her door I saw my daughter sitting on the couch talking on the cell phone like she was all grown up. Callie had her feet up on the coffee table, her hands resting on her belly. Jolene was rattling on explaining who Ryder was and why she loved him so much. Justin was on speakerphone so I could hear his end of the conversation. He loved the name but wanted to make sure it was unanimous. Jolene started giggling. "No, Uncle Justin. Not nanamous...it's Ryder." We all laughed at that. Jolene saw me standing at the door. "Mama, what's nanamous? Uncle Justin wants to name the baby nanamous."

I could barely breathe from laughing so hard. "No, baby..." I took a breath. "Not nanamous, u-nan-i-mous. It means we all like it. It's not the baby's name."

She smiled. "So he's Ryder, right?"

"Yes!" Callie said, "He's Ryder."

Jay came into the office. "So, we have a consensus?" We all started laughing and he looked around with confusion. I had tears streaming down my face from laughing. Unanimous, consensus. My child was bound to be so confused. Instead, Jolene sat holding the phone giggling until she snorted. That's my girl.

Callie spoke up. "Yes, Jay we do." Speaking into the phone she said, "Justin, honey? Should we use the other name we liked as the middle one now?"

"Sure, that sounds great. I'll let you guys hash all that out. I've got to get back to my meeting. Thanks for the laughs." He paused. "Babe, I love you."

Callie grinned. "I love you too. See you tonight." She made a kissy noise at the phone that cracked Jolene up again.

"Bye, Uncle Justin!" Jolene made kissy noises too. I shook my head. My child, what a ham.

I noticed Jay gesturing he wanted to speak to me. "I'll be right back, you two behave." Callie nodded while taking the phone. I heard her ask Jolene if she'd ever played the game with the birds. Oh boy, she'd opened up a can of worms now. I left hoping Callie had a full battery because Jolene would wear it out!

Jay was waiting in his office. I walked over and wrapped my arms around him. "We have some alone time. Jolene's playing with Callie's phone." Jay laughed knowing exactly what that meant. She'd taken his phone to her room one night when he stayed over. We'd found it by calling it the next morning. It was hidden under her bed with only one bar left on the battery. We were thankful we'd found it before it went completely dead.

"So, how does this weekend sound for our getaway? I just spoke with Gerry and we can use his cabin Friday and Saturday night." He kissed me gently waiting for my response.

"You're distracting me," I said between kisses. "You're not playing fair."

He chuckled. "Is it working?" He growled, still kissing me. "It's working for me." He said waggling his eyebrows.

I felt my skin tingle everywhere his lips touched. "I'm there. I just need to make sure it's okay with Callie."

He let me go pushing me gently toward the door. "Hurry back. I'm waiting." He grinned.

As I walked into Callie's office, she must've seen the flush on my cheeks. I started to speak but she interrupted. "Whatever it is, yes," she said laughing.

"Well, I was going to ask if you would take Jolene this weekend...like Friday and Saturday nights." I couldn't help grinning.

"Sure, sweets. Got it. Done deal. Now go tell your man. I'm sure he's anxious enough as it is." She dismissed me with a wave of her hand then turned her back to Jolene's game. "If you can get through this stage, you are my rock star!" Jolene had her tongue stuck out as she concentrated.

I practically danced back to Jay. I stopped outside the door and put on a serious face. His face lit up when he saw me but after seeing my expression he started pouting. "I'm sorry, Jay." I began. "You're going to have to put up with me all weekend." It took a moment for what I said to register then he smiled grabbing me in a hug, swinging me around. "You're making me dizzy!" I giggled.

"Just wait until this weekend, m'lady. You ain't seen nothing yet. I'd better get to work so we can leave early Friday." He gave me a quick kiss on the lips.

I floated back to my desk with a grin plastered on my face. I plopped onto my chair doing a mental inventory of all the things I'd need to take care of for Jolene before I went away. I pulled up a new word document and started making a list.

Chapter 13

For safety's sake, I kept Jolene at work with me for the rest of the week. I brought some of her DVDs and the portable player and she entertained herself while I worked. Jay and Callie were working hard on the designs for the Davenport project, and I didn't hear a single peep from Tyler. Jay had stayed at my apartment every night just in case he showed up, and I noticed that Jolene accepted our couch sharing without question. He was counting down to the weekend having marked Friday with a giant heart on the big calendar on the side of my fridge. One evening, before he'd gotten to my place, I carefully packed my weekend bag with my sexy lingerie and my love basket. I tucked my bag in the back of my closet so he wouldn't see it before we got ready to leave for the cabin. I packed Jolene's fairy princess luggage and made sure to throw several kid movies in just in case. Callie told me they were going to take her bumper bowling and to a movie to keep her busy, but I wasn't taking any chances. I kept bugging Jay about the cabin, what it looked like, did it have a hot tub. He wouldn't tell me a thing. He just smiled every time I asked and pretended to lock his mouth and throw away the key, much to the delight of my child who giggled every time he did it.

Friday morning came with us in our usual position, tangled on the couch. Jay gently brushed my hair back from my face and kissed my forehead. "Good morning, beautiful," he whispered. I cracked open one eye. "It's Friday, babe," he said smiling. Immediately, both eyes popped open. "I thought I'd get your attention with that piece of information," he said chuckling.

I sat up and rubbed my eyes. "Just think, no couch tonight," I said with a wink.

He furrowed his brows thinking. "I believe it has a really nice couch, if I remember correctly." My mouth fell open. "And a nice queen-sized bed, if you're so inclined." He started laughing as I poked him in the side.

"I'm going to get in the shower. You can make breakfast since you're being a bad boy this morning." I got up off the couch and padded into my room to grab my things. I heard Jolene run from her room telling Jay it was Friday and time for her special sleepover with Aunt Callie and Uncle Justin. She'd been so excited the night before that I almost gave her some cold medicine just to knock her out, but she'd eventually run out of steam on her own. I hopped in the shower taking extra time to make sure I wasn't sporting furry legs or underarms. I got out of the shower and with my heart beating faster with anticipation, I grabbed my special bag out of the closet. Just knowing that in a few hours I'd be modeling one of my outfits for Jay made my palms sweat. Why was I freaking out? We'd slept together so many times it was like second nature, but that was sleeping. I'd replayed our one and only night together so many times in my head and wondered if it was possible to surpass that night. Now I was going to find out. I took a deep breath, grabbed my bag and went to join Jay and Jolene for breakfast.

The workday seemed endless but finally it was time to leave for our weekend together. I'd never left Jolene that long before and was worried that she might get clingy and upset, but she was headed for the door with her bag as soon as Callie announced it was time to go. "Ahem, little lady?" I said watching her roll her bag along. "Are you going to give me a kiss goodbye, or not?" She stopped, ROLLED HER EYES, and came back to me. Oh, what these children pick up. I reached down, picked her up and gave her big smooches all over her face. "I'm going to miss you mini-me," I said as she squirmed in my arms.

She hugged me really hard and gave me a big wet kiss. "You'll be okay, Mama. I promise." I had to laugh. I put her down and she ran back to her bag, grabbed Callie's hand and started to pull her to the door.

"Call us if you have time!" Callie called over her shoulder as she was dragged out the door. "Have fun and don't worry!"

I felt Jay slip his hands around my waist pulling me back against him. He rested his chin on my shoulder. "You ready to roll?" He whispered. Just his whisper sent shivers through me. I nodded turning in his arms to face him. I was trembling with anticipation as he softly kissed me. "I'm ready, babe." We walked hand in hand to the car where he opened my door. After I was tucked in, he jogged around to his side. I found myself barely breathing thinking of the night ahead. We rode through Asheville and headed north. We literally had driven only about twenty minutes

when we turned toward Elk Mountain. Our
destination was on the side overlooking Asheville and
the Blue Ridge mountains. As we pulled up to the
cabin, my eyes grew wide. It was breathtaking. The
sun was starting to set and the sky was an amazing
palette of pink, orange and yellow. Jay opened my
door and I hesitated before getting out. "Is this real?"
I asked looking around in disbelief.

"Most definitely. Why don't you go ahead
inside. I'll get the bags. Gerry said he'd leave the key in
the door." He opened the trunk for our things as I
walked down the stone path to a wooden bridge which
crossed a tiny babbling brook. I stopped to look down
at the water rushing over the smooth stones and saw
koi and goldfish swimming in the pool among the reeds
that sprouted from the water. I heard Jay coming up
behind me, so I moved along to the wooden deck that
spanned the front of the cottage. A hot tub was
tucked in the corner and next to it were two rocking
chairs facing the view. A wall of French style doors
with matching windows gave the cottage an
unobstructed view of the mountains. I saw the key
hanging from the lock, I turned it and opened the door
leading into the living room. Jay came in behind me
pushing the door shut with his foot as his hands were

full. I jumped to help him but he shook his head and took them to our bedroom. *Our bedroom.* I noticed a rather inviting couch but it wasn't going to be used as our bed tonight. I took note of the generous kitchen and intimate dining table. Out of habit, I opened the fridge to see it was stocked with everything we'd need to make breakfast in the morning. I heard Jay moving around in the next room so I wandered in to see an ample sized bedroom with the queen bed as its centerpiece. A large picture window was next to the bed featuring a panoramic view. Jay had placed my bag on the bed and was unpacking his things. I noticed the bathroom was just off the bedroom and it had a huge glass block shower. There were robes and slippers for both of us laid out on the vanity. I'd never seen a place this beautiful in my life.

"Would you like to sit outside and have some wine?" Jay asked interrupting my daydreaming. "We could sit in the rocking chairs or even hit the hot tub. It's up to you."

I pondered for just a moment. "I think the hot tub sounds heavenly." I grabbed my bag and headed for the bathroom. "I'll just change and be right out."

"Sounds like a plan. I'll change too, grab the wine and meet you on the deck," he said springing into action.

I'd brought a sexy black bikini with me hoping there would be a pool or hot tub. As I slipped it on, I took a look in the mirror. My stomach had flattened out nicely after Jolene was born. Jay had already seen me in less than this, so I wasn't worried about covering up. I wanted to show him the sexier side of me. The queen of sweat pants needed a vacation. I slid my black kimono on as a cover-up in case it had gotten chilly. As I came out the door, I saw Jay sitting in the rocking chair. He had two glasses and an open bottle of wine sitting beside the hot tub. He'd also laid out towels within reach. He got up as he heard me shut the door. I let my eyes explore his chiseled chest and well-defined abs. He was wearing a pair of colorful board shorts that were hanging low on his hips showing off his narrow waist. He was checking me out as well. His eyes traveled up and down my body, taking in my very exposed legs and the deep v of the robe. "Well, hello," he said his voice gruff.

I couldn't resist teasing him. "You said bathing suits were optional, right?" I saw his eyes widen and his mouth fall open. I walked over, pushed his jaw closed with my fingers and gave him a soft kiss. His eyes were locked on me as I unbelted my robe letting it slip from my shoulders. I caught it as it fell and laid it across the back of the chair. If he was interested before he was VERY interested now that he'd seen the bikini. It was tiny triangles of fabric held together with strings and had been a treat for myself after the Victoria Secret shopping spree. I sauntered over to the hot tub to step gracefully in. That didn't happen. I slipped on the step and ended up completely submerging only to come up spluttering. I wiped my hair from my face and peeked open one eye to see Jay smiling at me. Not laughing, smiling. "You okay?" He asked.

"Yeah, not the sexiest entrance, I must say," I said laughing.

He started to step into the hot tub but at the last second, jumped in. I sat there looking at him with my mouth hanging open. "I can't let you have all the fun," he said laughing. He poured two glasses of wine and carefully sat back on the molded seat. I moved across to sit beside him. He handed me my glass then he slipped his hand around my waist to pull me close. I looked into his emerald green eyes and realized this is what love feels like. Being with a man who accepts you as you are, flaws and all. His look said it all. We sat together looking out at the mountains as the daylight faded, and we talked. I found out things I'd never known, things he'd never wanted to share before.

"I've always admired you, Jane. My mom raised me by herself and I know it's a hard and thankless job," he said taking a sip of wine. "Tyler reminds me a lot of my own father except my father's addiction wasn't drugs or alcohol. It was gambling and women."

"How old were you? When they split up, I mean?" I asked snuggling closer.

Jay's fingers were trailing up and down my side making me tingle. "I was old enough to know what it meant when they split up.   Thank God Tyler never got to do that damage to Jolene. In a way, he did her a favor by leaving before she was born," he said looking out at the now twinkling lights of Asheville. "I've never really gotten over it."

"Jay, we've been together a lot in the past few months but you've never told me this until now, why?"

I reached up to cup his chin, turning his face to look at me.

His eyes locked onto mine and he hesitated before speaking. "I think it's because I know in my heart that you love me. When I told you about Meredith, you didn't even blink. You looked upset but you turned it around and made me realize that I should've trusted you enough to tell you. You didn't leave and I don't think you would have. That's when I knew I could share who I really am with you...flaws and all." He kissed me gently on the lips.

I reached up to brush a piece of hair that had fallen across his eyes. "I don't see any flaws. You're a strong man who also has a kind heart. You've given my daughter an awesome example of what a good man should be. She'd never have had that with Tyler. I hope she never has to go through what I did." I set my wine glass down and reached up to cup his face with my hands. "Thank you for everything." I gently kissed him then pulled away. "I'm going to go in, dry off and slip into something sexier," I said as I climbed from the hot tub and used one of the fluffy towels to dry off.

His voice cracked. "I don't know how that's even possible," he said, again taking in my bikini.

I smiled giving him a wink. "I think it's my turn to say, baby, you ain't seen nothing yet." I picked up my robe and slipped it on to cut the chill of the night air. "I'll see you inside." He nodded with a smile. I sashayed into the cottage then dashed to the bedroom. I grabbed my bag, deposited my love basket on the side table, and headed into the bathroom. I needed to decide quickly which of my VS outfits was perfect for tonight. I looked in the bag and the one thing that screamed at me was the white bustier trimmed in black lace. As I slipped it on, I noticed for the first time what Callie had seen. I looked pretty hot! I finished getting dressed and pulled on the stockings making sure to attach them to the garters. As I slipped on my black stilettos I heard Jay rustling around in the bedroom. I put a dash of perfume on, brushed my teeth and fluffed my hair. I took a deep breath, one final glance in the mirror and opened the door.

Chapter 14

The first thing I noticed was the soft glow of candlelight and the next was the scent of roses. There were petals strewn around the room and on the bed. Jay was wearing a pair of pajama pants that hung low on his hips and he was holding a single rose. As I came into view I heard him growl his approval. I'd been so afraid of walking in the five inch heels, but I was as graceful as a runway model because my focus was on Jay, and I was totally calm. His eyes darkened with desire as he nodded his approval, taking me in from head to toe. He reached out his hand and I entwined my fingers with his. As he pulled me close, he stroked the rose softly against my cheek. I could smell the fragrant bloom, and I took a deep breath and closed my eyes. "I love what you're wearing," he whispered as he feathered kisses along my neck to finally nip gently at my earlobe. I turned my head and nuzzled his neck breathing in his musky scent as my tongue darted against his skin. I felt dizzy with desire. This time was different. We were in a different place emotionally and we both knew this was more than just a night together. "I love you, Jane," he said sliding his hand around to palm my lower back and pull me closer.

"I love you too," I said barely breathing. "So much."

My hands snaked into his hair, and I grasped him tightly pulling him into a slow, deliberate kiss. His fingers slid the strap of my bustier off my shoulder while placing a kiss in the hollow of my neck. I let my head fall back as he nuzzled my neck and his fingers traced up and down my spine. I watched as the candlelight made our shadows dance on the walls. Jay's fingers slid down my hips to reach the garters that held my stockings. Never taking his lips from my skin, I could feel his fingers unhooking them. His hands moved back to grasp my waist, and I noticed they were trembling. Wrapping me in his arms, he lifted me, and I wrapped my legs around his waist. I loved feeling his hard body pressed against me. His lips found mine, and I found my tongue darting out to taste the wine on his lips. I pulled myself tighter against him as his hands tangled in my hair. He kissed me harder, stealing my breath until I gasped. Holding me tightly, he lowered us to the bed. "I want to look at you, Jane," he whispered. Leaning away slightly, his gaze locked onto my own. I could feel the heat radiating from him as he gently placed his fingers on my neck letting them linger where my pulse was racing. He smiled then trailed his fingers down my bare skin causing me to shiver with anticipation. He kissed me lightly, his gaze focused on my exposed tummy. I held my breath, anxious for him to touch me again, but he hesitated then looked at me with a grin. "How did I miss this?" He growled pointing out my belly button piercing.

I smiled and batted my eyes. "I don't believe you were interested in my belly button last time and my graceful dive into the hot tub tonight probably distracted you."

"Well, I think it's hot!" He said touching it gently. "You've been holding out on me, Jane." He growled placing a tender kiss on my belly. His gaze traveled lower where he admired the tiny lace-trimmed panties that matched my bustier. He got up on his knees and moved toward my feet still clad in my stilettos. He cupped my calf and my ankle and slowly slid off my shoe. He grasped the silky stocking and slowly eased it off my leg, tossing it over his shoulder onto the floor. As he started to repeat the action with my other stocking, I leaned up on my elbows to watch him. He kissed my thigh where the top of the stocking began. As he slowly slid it down his mouth followed, stopping for a light kiss behind my knee, several on my calf and finally, the last on the arch of my foot. He climbed up to hover over me, and I couldn't resist grabbing him to pull him in for a deep passionate kiss. I managed to roll him over onto his back and I ended up straddling him, never breaking the kiss. I finally broke away and saw the surprise on his face as I was taking charge now. I leaned down to nuzzle his neck, my hair trailing over his skin and I heard him moan. I used my tongue to lick his collarbone as my hands explored the soft skin of his chest. He watched me, his eyes intense. My hands were greedy for more, so I slid them down his chiseled abs. Groaning, he grabbed me rolling me back onto the bed. "You are trying to kill me, aren't you?" He said breathlessly.

I looked at this man who had stolen my heart. "No way, baby. I need you," I whispered.

He smiled. "I need you too. You have no idea how much," he said before his mouth closed over mine. His hands slipped down the side of my bustier and I felt the zipper slowly lowering. I felt his fingers brush my bare skin. I slid my hand up his side feeling every ripple of muscle as he held himself tensed above me. He tugged my bustier off. I felt the cool air caress my skin. I could feel his eyes devouring me as he closed his mouth over mine for another searing kiss. I felt his hand slipping my panties down. A moment later, leaving me breathless, he scooted down the bed to draw them completely off, tossing them alongside my bustier. He then ran his hands up my bare legs, hips, and sides causing me to tremble with excitement. Once again, he captured my mouth with a heated kiss as he tangled his hands in my hair.

"I'll be right back," he whispered moving to the bedside table to steal a treasure from my basket. I closed my eyes and sighed feeling the soft sheets against my skin. I felt the bed move as he joined me and I could feel his bare legs tangling with mine. My head was spinning from the sensations of our bodies touching, our breaths mingling and our hearts beating as one. It was as if we had always been lovers, our bodies so familiar, so right. Every nerve ending in my body was tingling, and I felt as if I was on fire. I grasped his shoulder with one hand while wrapping my fingers into his hair, pulling him to me for another intense kiss. Breathlessly, I cried out as he held me in his strong arms, and I closed my eyes as I felt myself fragment into a million pieces. Within moments, I heard him moan my name as we both crashed back to earth, our bodies exhausted.

I opened my eyes to see him studying my face. "You are so beautiful. I can't believe you're mine," he said tenderly cupping my face.

I lightly traced my fingers down his cheek. "You've got me, as long as you want me," I said softly.

He smiled. "How does forever sound?" He brushed my hair from my eyes.

I giggled. "It sounds good to me." I waited for him to laugh, but he didn't, instead his expression grew serious. "Jane, I do want forever. I've been feeling this way for a long time, but had to be sure you felt the same way. I love Jolene too and want us to be a family. I want us to be together."

I felt tears in my eyes as I saw the love glowing in his. "Jay, I—"

"Before you say anything, let me do this right." He leaned over the side of the bed, sat back up and held out a tiny box. I could feel my heart hammering as I looked at the box then up at Jay. I sat up pulling the sheet around me. He took my hand and looking into my eyes he said, "From the first day I saw you hiding behind the couch in Callie's office almost a year ago, I knew you were something special. When you told me about Jolene and how you were raising her on your own, I felt so connected with you." He tucked a piece of hair behind my ear. "Babe, you've shown me what it's like to have a family and those few days we were apart, I missed you so much it hurt." My bottom lip was trembling so he leaned forward to softly kiss me. "I want to be your husband. I want to be Jolene's daddy and I want us to have our own beautiful kids one day."

He cracked open the box to reveal a gorgeous princess cut diamond ring. My mouth fell open as I looked from the ring back up to him. "Jay, are you sure?"

"I'm so sure. I've never been so sure of anything in my life. I've been dreaming of this moment for a while. If you need time to think about this, I understand, but I have to ask. Jane Victoria Carter, will you marry me?"

I looked into his eyes and saw all the love I could ever ask for. I held out my left hand and I saw him begin to smile. "Jay, I'd be honored to marry you," I said my voice breaking.

He took the ring from the box and slipped it on my finger. "And I promise to love you forever." He leaned forward capturing my mouth in a tender kiss, slid back under the sheets and wrapped me in his arms.

As I lay there thinking about his proposal, I realized that he'd seriously been planning this for a long time. He'd brought a ring with him that had obviously been fitted since it was exactly my size. I curled into the crook of his arm laying my hand across his chest I listened to his heart beating. He absently twirled my hair between his fingers then he gently kissed the top of my head. "Jay? I said softly.

"Yeah babe?" He murmured sleepily.

"Did Callie and Justin know you were going to ask me?" I just had to know.

He shifted to look at me. "No, I didn't tell anyone...except I did ask Jolene."

I raised myself up on my elbow to rest my chin on his chest. "What did she think of this?" I asked, imagining how that went down.

He chuckled. "First she squealed. That was a given. Then she looked at me very seriously and said, 'You have to live happy ever after.' She was right. I do want my happy ever after."

My child, what an old soul. I was so happy he'd asked her and it made me melt thinking about how much she loved him. "I want mine too, Jay."

His gaze locked onto mine, he growled, "You ain't seen nothing yet." He rolled me back, his body pressing against mine. He gave me a fiery kiss full of promise, love and passion.

The next morning, the sun was already pretty high in the sky when we awoke. Exhausted from the night before, we'd slept in and I realized I needed to check in on Jolene. I could hear Jay's even breathing. Not wanting to wake him, I crept out of bed, grabbed my phone and headed into the bathroom. I looked in the mirror as I slipped on my fluffy robe and slippers they'd provided and saw my ring catch the light. It really hadn't been a dream. We were engaged! I wanted to tell Callie but also didn't think a text or phone call was the way to do it. If Jolene hadn't spilled the beans about Jay's conversation with her then it was still a secret. I decided to wait until I got home to tell her. I checked my phone to see no missed calls, just a text from Callie from the night before.

10pm check in. Jolene safely in bed. Justin and I exhausted. She wore our asses out! Hope you are having fun! Love you!

I had to laugh. They were just boarding the exhaustion train. It was going to be the non-stop to California when little Ryder made his appearance. Jolene was a piece of cake compared to the demands of a baby. Suddenly, I remembered what Jay said about having kids one day, and I felt my body flush. A baby with Jay, a child of our own. The thought of a baby being brought into the world with both parents loving it and being a part of its life made tears spring to my eyes. Jolene would be an awesome big sister too. I was so lost in thought I jumped when there was a knock at thedoor. Opening the door quickly, I found Jay standing there naked with his hair mussed up. I was so overcome by everything. I grabbed his face and gave him a big, wet kiss. "Good morning!" I said watching a big smile spread across his face.

"Do you promise to give me a kiss like that every morning, for as long as we both shall live?" He said with a wink.

I wrapped my arms around his neck and said enthusiastically, "I do!"

I felt him untying the belt of my robe which he quickly slipped off my shoulders. He started walking me backwards until we were in the shower then he turned on the water. No words were needed as we stood together, our bodies under the warm stream from the rain showerhead. He reached past me to grab the shampoo, squeezed some into his palm and began massaging it into my damp hair. His fingertips made my scalp tingle, and I could smell the fragrance of coconuts from the lather that was now streaming down my body. When he was finished, he walked me back under the spray, his hands never leaving my wet skin. He covered a wash cloth in body wash and began gently washing my neck, my shoulders and my back in soft circles. "This has been my fantasy for a long time," he said softly. I turned to face him letting the water wash the soap away. I took the washcloth from him and began to wash his muscular chest and abdomen. He took the washcloth from me, dropped it on the tile and in one motion, scooped me up dripping wet. "Woman, you are irresistible. I'm taking you back to bed."

Chapter 15

We spent most of the day in bed, only taking a break to grab some food and then jumping right back in again. As evening approached, we were wrapped up in a blanket sitting side by side on the deck watching the sky change with all its vibrant colors. Jay had his arm around me holding me close. I looked up at him and saw he had the most content smile I'd ever seen. I snuggled in closer and sighed, "I could stay here forever."

He kissed my forehead softly. "I would love that but reality is calling us back home tomorrow. Who knows, one day we might own a place like this of our own and we can come up to get away from it all."

"Speaking of reality," I said starting to get up. "I need to check my phone to see if there are any more messages from Callie." He got up with me and we shuffled back into the cottage still wrapped in the blanket. "You know what? Callie's going to be mad if she finds out I only wore one of my outfits." I left him with the blanket on the couch while I went in search of my phone.

His eyes never left me. "Well, truthfully, I loved unwrapping the package but I love seeing you the way you are right now even better," he said waggling his eyebrows.

"You are insatiable!" I said laughing. I found my phone and saw several missed calls from a number I didn't recognize. I checked my texts and there were a couple from Callie.

Don't panic, call me. Not Jolene.

Jane, call me asap.

I looked up at Jay. "Something's wrong at home. Callie texted me to call her. I have a bad feeling about this."

Jay jumped up to come stand beside me. "You can't think the worst. Call her and see what's up." He looked at the messages. "She said not to panic."

With shaking hands, I called Callie. I put her on speakerphone. She answered on the first ring. "Hey, quit freaking out. I know you are," she said, before I could say anything.

"Ok, I'm trying not to freak out. What's going on?" I said as Jay put his arm around me to calm me.

"Did you get a call from your landlord? Or did you ignore him too?" She asked.

"My landlord? Oh wait, the missed calls. I didn't recognize the number. Why what's happened?" Now I was thinking fire. All of Jolene's baby pictures, our things that couldn't be replaced.

"It wasn't a fire, if that's what you're thinking. It was a break-in."

I was stunned. A break-in? We lived in a great area, how could this happen? "How bad is it?" I asked fearing my electronics were now gone along with any jewelry that had any value.

"Well, the burglar only rummaged through your room. Your drawers were dumped out and your clothes were tossed all over the room. The rest of the place wasn't touched. They broke in through the window in your bedroom and it's possible something scared them off before they could get anything else." She paused. "I thank God you guys weren't home when they broke in."

I took a deep breath. She was right, we were so lucky that we weren't home but who would want to break in? I really didn't have anything of value. The only thing that meant the world to me was Jolene. Jay spoke up. "Callie, we're coming back now. We'll come by your place to pick up Jolene and then I'll run Jane by her apartment to pick up some things. They'll be staying at my place for a while."

Callie sounded relieved. "Oh that's perfect. I was going to offer for you guys to stay over here but we're going to be having our spare room made into the nursery."

Jay said, "I have plenty of room in my house. It makes more sense for them to stay with me." He pulled me close and I lay my head on his chest.

I knew he was right, and I wasn't going to argue but something kept nagging at me about the break-in. "Callie, did the police find any fingerprints or anything that might give them a clue about who did this?"

"I asked them that too, but they said whoever it was, was wearing gloves so no fingerprints. Umm…Jane, you don't think it was Tyler, do you?" Callie asked nervously.

I didn't want to believe Tyler would resort to that to get to me, but I really wasn't sure. Maegan had described the drunken guy who was beating on my door and it sounded just like Tyler, but I had no concrete proof. Now I'd had a break-in and the only things they messed with were mine. "Callie, I don't know…I just don't know. You guys keep Jolene with you until we get back. We'll pack and head back now."

"Ok, Justin and I are both home with Jolene so don't worry about her. You guys just be safe coming back," Callie said before hanging up.

I looked up at Jay. "This is scaring me. I don't think Tyler would be stupid enough to break into my apartment but I really don't know him anymore." I took a shaky breath feeling the tears coming.

Jay kissed me gently. "Babe, let's head home and get Jolene. I know you're worried most about that." He sprinted to the bedroom to get started packing.

"Jay, wait." He stopped at the doorway, turning with a confused look. I wrapped my arms around his neck giving him a kiss. "Thank you for loving us. I'm so lucky to have you."

He looked into my eyes. "Jane, I'm the lucky one," he said wrapping his arms around me. "I'm afraid you're stuck with me for life."

"I'm glad. I can't imagine my life without you." I kissed him tenderly. "Now let's go get our girl."

We grabbed our clothes and stuffed them in the bags. Within thirty minutes we were packed and on the road. When we pulled up at Callie's, I saw her peeking out of the curtains. We got out, and I was about to ring the buzzer when the door unlocked for us. We went upstairs and saw Callie standing outside in the hall. She looked around to make sure Jolene wasn't behind her before she whispered. "I'm not sure, but I looked out earlier and thought I saw Tyler across the street."

Jay tensed beside me. "Are you kidding me?" His face grew red. "If he's out there, I'm going to kick his ass up and down the street." I saw him ball his fists, so I put my hand on his arm to calm him. He started to go back downstairs but Callie called him back.

"Jay, I don't know for sure. Don't go out there. Jolene doesn't know anything about the break in and I don't want her to see you pounding some guy in the street."

He stopped, took a deep breath then turned to come back up. "You're right. I don't want that." He wrapped his arm around my shoulders and I snuggled into his side while resting my hand on his chest.

"OH MY GOD!" Callie screamed. "Is that an engagement ring?!" She grabbed my hand pulling it to her for closer inspection.

"Yes, I wanted to tell you yesterday but I waited to tell you in person," I said laughing as she turned my finger every which way but loose.

"Jay, you did good!" She said smiling. "I assume since you're wearing it, you said yes." She laughed.

Jay spoke before I could. "Of course she said yes! I'm irresistible!" He leaned down to give me a gentle kiss.

"He's kind of hard to resist, I'll admit," I said poking him in the side. "And very modest as well."

The door to the condo opened and Jolene came flying out. "Mama! Jay! You're home! Jay did you ask Mama if you could engage with her?" She said looking up at the both of us with the biggest smile on her face.

I knelt down and held my hand out to show her the ring. "What do you think about this present Jay got me for being engaged?"

Her mouth fell open as she took her finger and touched the stone. "Jay, I want one! Can I have one too?" She started jumping up and down grabbing Jay by the hand. He reached down to pick her up and she wrapped her arms around his neck.

"Sweet Pea, I will get you one that you can wear when we get married. How's that sound?" He said giving her a hug.

He leaned his head toward her and she leaned in to touch her forehead to his and they looked eye to eye. She suddenly said, "Are you going to be my daddy?"

We all stood looking at her dumbfounded for a moment then Jay spoke directly to her. "Jolene, I would love to be your daddy, if you want me to be."

Keeping her forehead touching his, she said, "I love you and want you to engage me too. Can we all live in the same house?"

We all started laughing and I hugged both her and Jay. "Yes, baby, Jay's going to let us live with him." I heard sniffling and turned to see Callie crying. I wrapped her in my hug too. "Are you okay?" I asked.

Tears rolling down her cheeks, she sobbed, "Yes, I'm just so happy." I looked at Jay over her head and mouthed 'hormones.' He nodded with a knowing smile.

Mrs. Callahan poked her head out of her door holding her little poodle. "Everything all right out here?" She said taking in Jay holding Jolene who were both laughing and Callie crying.

"Yes, Mrs. Callahan," I said smiling. "Everything's just fine. We've just got a lot going on."

Jolene spoke up, "Ms. Callahan, Jay's gonna engage my mama and me and be my daddy and we're gonna live in his big house."

Mrs. Callahan looked at me and smiled. "I guess I'll need to call Officer Taylor and tell him you've been a bad girl," she said with a wink as she passed by to take her dog out.

Jay looked at me with a confused look. I made sure she was out of earshot and said, "Who knows what she's talking about...she's a mess, bless her heart."

Chapter 16

As we arrived at my apartment, Maegan came barreling out the door to greet us. I gave Jay the key and told him to go ahead and take Jolene straight to her room. I didn't want to make her afraid by seeing my room.

As Jay shut the door, Maegan said, "What in the world is going on? I heard breaking glass last night so I got Nate up to take a look. He turned on the porch light but didn't see anything. He went out this morning and saw your back window busted in."

Just then Maegan's husband poked his head out the door. I could hear the triplets squealing in the background. "Hey, Jane. I wanted to let you know that I fixed the window with a piece of plywood since the landlord wasn't gonna get to it until later tonight."

"Thanks so much, Nate. At least they wouldn't get back in easily," I said gratefully.

"So," Maegan asked. "What are you gonna do now?" She looked so worried so I let her in on where we were going.

"We're going to stay with Jay for a while. Jay thinks it's safer," I explained.

"Well, I'm gonna keep an eye on your place for you," Nate said looking around suspiciously. "Somebody messes with my friends, they mess with me."

"I appreciate that so much, Nate. I don't know what we'll do. Since Jay and I are engaged now, this may be us moving in with him for good."

Maegan's eyes grew wide. "You're engaged! Oh my gosh! Congratulations, hun." She gave me a hug. "You deserve some happiness and so does Jolene. I'm so happy for y'all."

"Thanks," I said smiling. "This is something I've dreamed of for a long time." I heard the door open and Jay was signaling to me. "Hey, I'll call you after we get settled." I assured Maegan. "I need to get my stuff packed." Nodding, she and Nate opened the door, I heard squealing and then silence as it closed.

Jay was standing there waiting. As he pulled me close he whispered, "I think this was Tyler's doing."

"What makes you say that?" I said, fearful of what he'd found.

"Well, I went in your room to look around and it's all your personal stuff that's been trashed. It looks like the person who did this had a beef with you and in my opinion that can only mean Tyler. I'll be glad when you're out of here and safely at my house. I've got an alarm system and I'll feel better knowing you'll be there with me."

"I agree. Hey, can you keep Jolene busy for a few minutes while I see what my bedroom looks like?" I said giving him a kiss.

"Sure, babe. Just don't be long. I want to get you both as far away from here as possible," he said heading to Jolene's room.

I walked into my bedroom and felt sick to my stomach. My room looked like a tornado had gone through it. My bed was messed up, the nightstand drawer was dumped out on the bed and the entire contents of my dresser were strewn across the floor. My closet door was hanging off the track and everything that had been hung neatly was now lying in a pile on the floor with the hangers all tangled together. I just stood there stunned. Could Tyler have done this? Jay was right, it did look very personal. It almost looked like whoever had done this was looking for something, something intimate that would be hidden among my personal things. I started to pick up some of my clothes to put them back on the hangers but ended up dropping them. I couldn't do it. I felt so violated and it pissed me off. I started throwing the clothes in a pile on the bed. I pulled back the comforter to straighten it and my heart leapt into my throat. Laid out perfectly under it was Tyler's sweatshirt. I started to throw it but common sense took hold. I pulled out my phone and took a picture of it and the rest of the room. I balled up the shirt and tossed it across the room then took a duffle bag from the closet and started stuffing my things into it. I went into my bathroom to get my makeup. The medicine cabinet door was open but when I pushed it closed I saw written in lipstick:

THIS IS THE HARD WAY!

I heard Jay knock on the bedroom door. "Jane, you okay?" He asked softly.

I didn't answer right away so he came looking for me and found me staring at the mirror. He followed my gaze to see the words that now squeezed my heart like a vise. "It was him. Son of a bitch."

His voice brought me back. I looked at him and realized I needed to get Jolene as far away from this apartment as possible. "Jay, can you get my stuff off of the bed? I want to get out of here." I realized my hands were trembling as I scooped the contents of my vanity into my makeup bag. I snapped a quick picture of the mirror to add to my evidence. Jay grabbed my bag, stopping to take note of how I'd crammed everything in it. He walked back over to me, dropped it and wrapped his arms around me.

"Babe, let's go home," he said kissing my forehead. He reached down, scooped up my bag, took my hand and we walked out to get Jolene. As we got close to her room, we could hear her talking. I opened her door and she was at her window waving at someone.

"Jolene, honey? What are you doing?" I asked getting her attention away from the window.

"Mr. Tyler was outside. He wanted to take me to the movies but I told him he was a stranger and I don't go with strangers because Mama said so," she said matter-of-factly. Jay moved so fast he was at the window in a flash. He put Jolene behind him as he looked outside. "Did I do good Mama? You said Mr. Tyler was a stranger, right?"

I ran over to grab her in a hug. "Yes baby, you did really good." I could feel myself wanting to cry but didn't want to scare her. "We don't want Mr. Tyler coming to see you any more so we're going to leave right now. Do you have all your things you want to take?" I looked around her room and saw she'd packed her bag with her underwear, socks and Rapunzel. I grabbed a handful of clothes out of her drawer and stuffed them in the duffle that held my clothes. Jay turned from the window with a thunderous expression. "Jolene, run to your bathroom and get your toothbrush, okay?" I said to get her out of the room for a moment. She skipped out of the room and as soon as she was out of hearing I said, "Did he think he was going to kidnap her? Has he lost his freaking mind? Do you think we should call the police?"

Jay took a deep breath. "I still think he wants Jolene as leverage. He wants a payoff, I'm sure of it. What would he do with a child who doesn't even know who he is? He can't take care of himself, never mind a child. The police won't believe Jolene anyway."

"What are we going to do?" I said softly trying not to let Jolene hear us.

"We're just going to have to see what his next move is," he said with his jaw clenched. "I swear, we'll fight him. He's not going to get Jolene."

Chapter 17

They say that children can adapt to anything, and I believe it. I was worried that Jolene wouldn't be comfortable in a strange place, but as soon as she walked through the door she asked which room was hers. Jay had a really spacious three-bedroom house that he'd explained was really more of an investment than anything since he'd been single with no plans to get married or have a family when he bought it. It was a really beautiful house and I could totally see us living there as a family. Jolene ran from room to room looking at everything and she squealed with delight when she saw the huge garden tub in the master bathroom. "Can I swim in your pool?" She asked mesmerized by the sheer size of the tub.

Jay laughed. "Sweet Pea, it's a bathtub, not a pool, but I'm sure we can let you take a bath in it with lots of bubbles."

She clapped her hands and ran to the next room which happened to be the master bedroom. She threw herself onto the king sized bed and began bouncing up and down like she was on a trampoline. "Is this where you and Mama will sleep?" She asked slightly out of breath from her exertions.

I looked at Jay and saw his eyebrows were raised. I decided to see if this was going to be accepted. "Do you think this is where Jay and I should sleep?" I asked, watching her giggle as she threw herself onto the bed.

"Yes, Mama. The couch is too small. This bed is nenormous!." She lay down in the middle of the bed with her arms spread out like she was making snow angels.

Jay chuckled. "I guess we just got upgraded." He took my bag and set it next to the bed. "We get the nenormous bed."

I looked at my daughter and realized that despite my trying to protect her, my child wasn't stupid and she'd obviously put two and two together about Jay and me sharing the couch like a bed. So much for putting on appearances.

Jay walked over to stand at the door. "Jolene, I think I know the perfect room for you. Come on, Sweet Pea." She stopped bouncing immediately, sat down and climbed off the bed. He took her hand and they walked off down the hall. Curious, I followed to find them at the door of a room done in soft pastel pink. There was a white canopy bed in the middle of the room that was covered in stuffed toys and dolls. A white wicker table and chairs were set up all ready for tea parties. I stood there staring in disbelief. Jay turned his face breaking into a smile. "A few weeks ago I told my mom all about you and Jolene and that I was going to propose. I was hoping you'd say yes. Mom is dying to meet you both. I told her I needed help fixing up a room for a little princess, so she came over and helped me." Jolene was standing with her mouth open looking up at Jay.

"This is my room?" She said in disbelief. "I can keep it?" She turned to look at me. "Please Mama, can I keep it?"

"Of course you can keep it," I said smiling, blinking back tears. She squealed and ran into the room throwing herself onto the bed. Jay walked back to me and took my hand. Hand in hand we watched

Jolene investigate the toys and dolls on the bed. "You're too good to us," I said softly.

Jay lifted my hand to his lips placing a gentle kiss to my skin. "You deserve so much more," he whispered then placed another kiss on my hand. "I love you, Jane." I sighed. The man had my heart.

Jolene hopped off the bed and dashed out to the living room. "This house is so big!" She said running in circles around the room. "Is this all our house?"

Jay looked at me and laughed. "I guess it's a little bigger than your apartment." As Jolene ran by he said, "Sweet Pea. I want this to be your house."

She stopped suddenly. Breathlessly, she ran to Jay and gave him a hug. "I love you." She yawned and I took note of the time.

"I think someone's ready for bed. Let's get you in the bath and your jammies," I said taking her by the hand.

"Can I take my bath in the bubble tub?" She asked wide-eyed.

Jay knelt down in front of her. "Yes, but you can only go in the bubble tub when one of us is with you. Will you promise me?" She nodded solemnly.

Jay ran the tub, but we found no bubble bath in the house. I looked at my child pouting so I took some body wash, squeezed a big dollop in and turned on the jets. Within moments, the tub was full of soft foamy bubbles. Jolene climbed in with my help and disappeared in the cloud. We were laughing when Jay walked in.

"Where'd Jolene go?" He said pretending to look around. She stayed hidden in the bubbles giggling. "Jane, did she leave?"

"You know, I don't know where she went," I said seriously.

Suddenly, she burst from the foam. "Surprise!" She said throwing bubbles all over the walls and floor. I cringed seeing the mess all over the bathroom.

Instead of being angry about the mess, Jay started laughing. "Wow, you really scared me! I thought you were a bubble monster!" That made Jolene giggle even harder. I sat there holding the towel realizing I couldn't stop smiling. Our life was going to be so different. Seeing them together made me realize we were going to be a real family. I silently prayed that nothing would happen to change that. I got my slippery child dried off, blow dried her hair, and tucked her in her new bed. She looked so adorable surrounded by the mob of stuffed toys that she refused to take off the bed. Jay and I each gave her a goodnight kiss, told her we loved her, and wished her sweet dreams. I swear she fell asleep with a smile on her face.

We walked into the living room and sat together on the large oversized sofa. I curled up under his arm snuggling into his chest. He softly kissed my forehead and laid his cheek against the top of my head. We sat watching our favorite sitcom "Big Bang Theory" and I found myself laughing out loud at Sheldon's antics. Jay looked at me tenderly. "I remember sitting with you just like this, watching you laugh, and falling in love with you," he whispered. Just his whisper sets me aflame. I placed my hand on his cheek and pulled him to me, my lips hungrily seeking his.   When we finally broke the kiss, both of us were breathless. He stood, took me by the hand and took me to our bedroom.

Chapter 18

The next morning, the warmth of the sun streaming through the blinds woke me. I felt the gentle weight of Jay's arm lying across me and the warmth of his body against my back. I lifted my head to look at the clock on the bedside table and saw it was almost seven. I heard a tiny knock at the door a moment later. "Come in, sweetie," I said softly, trying not to wake Jay.

The door burst open and Jolene came bounding in and jumped on the bed on top of Jay. I heard him grunt and struggle for a moment before he realized it was her. I couldn't help but laugh. He lifted his head to look see her giggling at him.

"What's so funny, Sweet Pea?" He said clearing his throat of his gravelly morning voice as he turned over.

"Your hair's funny. It's sticking up like a porkopine," she said touching it with her hand. He ran his hands through his hair and laughed.

"Well this porkopine's going to tickle a certain Sweet Pea," he said pulling her up between us. I held her while he tickled under her chin until she squealed. When she finally settled down, we lazed around for a little bit longer. I knew we needed to get moving if we were going to get to work on time. We'd agreed Jolene would go to work with us until we could check out some day care centers closer to Jay's house. I hated to uproot her from where she'd been since she was a baby but since Tyler had figured out where she was, I wasn't taking any chances. While Jolene was in her room getting dressed, I called and explained the situation to Mrs. Bloom. She was totally understanding about everything and even suggested another daycare. While I was on the phone, Jay opened the bathroom door, in his towel, to let the steam from the shower out. I found myself checking him out while I spoke. He stopped, flexed his muscles and threw me a sexy wink. Stifling a giggle, I thanked Mrs. Bloom for all they'd done for Jolene and me through the years. I was just about to say goodbye when Jay dropped the towel. I told Mrs. Bloom thank you and hung up the phone. I dashed into the bathroom and locked the door. Jay was grinning when I leaned my back against the door.

"Something you need?" He asked innocently. I walked up behind him and trailed my fingers starting at his hip and up to his shoulder. I tangled my fingers in his hair and pulled him in for a searing kiss.

"No, just looking," I said walking away leaving him slack-jawed. "Two can play that game, Mister," I said laughing. He grabbed his towel and tried to snap it at me, but I was faster than he expected. "Get dressed, Mr. Anderson. You have to get to work. No time to play right now...but I think I can fit you in later," I said giving him an exaggerated wink.

"You're going to owe me, woman," he said shaking his head as he went back into the bathroom to finish getting ready.

All of us finally got ready and rode to the office. Callie's car was parked in the lot alongside Justin's. "Did you know Justin was coming today?" I asked as I unsnapped Jolene from her booster seat.

"No, I thought he was going to be in Charlotte," Jay said grabbing Jolene's bag from the car.

Jolene hopped out of the car and suddenly yelled, "Wait, Daddy!" She ran over, grabbing his hand to walk in with him. Jay stopped and looked at her with the biggest smile on his face. I loved it! She had done that completely on her own and that made it even more special. They stood on the sidewalk to wait for me, but I waved for them to go ahead. They walked up the steps to the building, and I unlocked the trunk to get my laptop bag. A noise behind me made me whip my head around. A strange man was standing behind me and I found myself backing against the car.

"Can I help you?" I said startled that I hadn't seen him when we pulled up.

"You Jane Carter?" He looked me up and down and it gave me the creeps. I was wishing now that I'd made Jay wait with me.

"Yes, again...can I help you...Mr.?"

"You don't need to know my name. Tyler said I'm supposed to deliver a message." He reached in his coat pocket, and I felt my heart stop. All I could think was he was going to hurt me, and I was just feet from my child and the man I loved. I watched as he pulled out an envelope and handed it to me. With shaking hands, I took it from him.

"Have a nice day," he said with a leering glance. He turned and walked away.

I slumped against the car with relief, my body trembling. I heard Jay call my name but I was still shaken and couldn't speak. He came running around the car to find me leaning against the door.

"Babe. What in the hell happened? Are you okay?" He was holding my shoulders looking me over closely to make sure I wasn't hurt. It took me a moment to speak. I looked into his eyes and the tears just started flowing down my cheeks. He pulled me tightly to him. "Jane, what happened, you have to tell me. Oh my God, you're trembling. Babe, you're scaring me."

I finally was able to take a breath. I held up the envelope and he took it from me, while still wrapping his arm around me to hold me up. "He said Tyler sent him," I whispered. "Jay, I thought he was going to hurt me. I was so scared."

"Let's get you inside and we'll see what this is." He wrapped his arm around me to walk me inside. Jay walked me over to the reception couch and sat me down. Jolene was watching her DVD player at his desk and hadn't noticed anything unusual which relieved my mind a little. Callie and Justin were walking out of her office when they saw my face and came running over.

"What happened?" Callie said sitting down next to me. She grabbed my hand which was still shaking and put her arm around my shoulders.

Jay looked at Justin. "Some creep in the parking lot came up behind her and handed her this envelope." They both looked at the writing on it, and I saw Jay's expression darken. "Jane, do you want me to open it?" He said giving Justin a look I didn't understand.

I was so shaken I knew I couldn't open it. "Yes, please, what is it?" He ripped open the envelope and scanned the paper quickly. He passed it to Justin whose expression now matched Jay's. "What is it?" I started to freak out again.

Jay sat on the coffee table in front of me. "Apparently, Tyler got a lawyer and he's demanding a DNA test. He's trying to get custody of Jolene."

I stopped trembling with fear and was now vibrating with anger. I looked at Jolene, my child. She is the child I carried, gave birth to, and raised by myself. I stood up, looked at my fiancé and friends and said with conviction, my voice strong. "Well, he'd better be prepared for a fight."

To be continued:

Forever by Design

Early Summer 2013

www.ingramcontent.com/pod-product-compliance
Lightning Source LLC
Chambersburg PA
CBHW070821120626
46556CB00002B/612